# At the Hands of Others

By
Barry S. Jandebeur

Published by Piscataqua Press
An imprint of RiverRun Bookstore, Inc.
142 Fleet Street | Portsmouth, NH | 03801
www.riverrunbookstore.com
www.piscataquapress.com

ISBN: 978-1-944393-11-3

Printed in the United States of America

*In Memoriam*

❧

LCDR Harold E. Jandebeur
United States Navy Retired
"An officer and a gentleman"

August 4, 1918–February 10, 2015

## Acknowledgments

Some time ago, I gathered a special group of trusted individuals. Not to praise me or make me feel good, but to be straightforward and honest. They are my first readers, but they are much more. Coming from myriad walks of life, they provide a crucial window into my reader's minds by bringing to the process extraordinary feedback and critique.

My wife, Diane, forever my confidant and best friend, remains a captured audience who may read my stories as many times as I do. She is both in-house critic and primary first reader with skills and attention to the task that I count on and appreciate more and more as we continue this journey together.

My ever faithful friends, Jon and Bonnie Nelson, listen, read and tolerate the steps that get my work ready. They provide valued support and direction through to publication and beyond.

Fred Holmberg, my poet and writer friend, sits me down and with his notes in hand takes me carefully through his thoughts and critique keeping me sharp and on point.

Cathy Breen graciously accepted my invitation to be my newest first reader. With a dedicated eye and caring demeanor, she meets my characters, engages with them, inhabits their sense of place and then provides me with a crisp report. She is an extraordinary, appreciated addition to my process.

In the end, the manuscript took a trip to New Gloucester, Maine where it spent quality time in the hands of my manuscript consultant, Joan Dempsey. Joan is a dynamic and crucial part of my process. I often wonder how I was "getting by" before. She guides me with a firm but gentle hand and with her professional eye holds me ever accountable. The end story I share with readers is richer because of her.

I thank all for their interest and incredible support. Their keen and willing eyes remain one of my most valued tools.

## A Note from the Author

Sometimes it is at our weakest moments that we find our greatest power.

Being strong doesn't mean you don't fear things it just means you fear them in a different way.

As alone as we might feel at times, we are always but one of many that make up the warmth and compassion of our community of man. When we embrace the whole that we are a part of, our lives are enriched by what we learn and gain at the hands of others.

"Writing a novel is like driving a car at night.

You can only see as far as your headlights, but

You can make the whole trip that way."


~ E.L. Doctorow ~


"I think life is like that:

we can only see so far ahead at any time."


~ Togquos ~

# CHAPTER ONE
## *Call me Jonathan*

*I*'d like to start at the beginning, but I don't know the beginning. I know the middle and the beginning of the end, but as mere fragments, a kaleidoscope of shards falling together only to fly apart, leaving me with as many questions as answers.

I must have a name, but I don't know what it is, where I'm from or why I found myself in the middle of the woods. All I know is that I woke up, not in the sense of having been asleep, but with an awareness that I existed. I suspect it must be similar to coming out of a coma.

I didn't appear to be injured, only groggy and achy. Other than a persistent itch around my mouth and nose that had me repeatedly drawing the back of my hand across my face, I seemed fine. I had a watch on my left wrist and there was an indentation and white trail on my tanned third finger; I must have worn a ring. I had no wallet, no identification and what I found in my pockets included a nickel, three pennies, and a small pocket knife marked "Gerber," which had an open frame construction. I also had a tube of Chap Stick, and a sealed packet labeled "Vision Clear," for cleaning eye glasses. On a stump a pair of glasses lay folded properly, waiting. I put them on.

I wore khaki shorts and what appeared to be rugged hiking boots. My tanned legs suggested this to be my regular attire. The warmth of the day penetrated the canopy of high pine trees and the synthetic material of my blue T shirt felt cool against my skin. My mind flashed like a slide show playing in rapid motion, but nothing except a fleeting image that faded as quickly as it came twisted into focus. An image of me turning and waving and then walking down a path. I walked with a stick that I swung ahead of me. I looked back to say something, but all I get is "I'll make it..." In the white haze, a woman waved, then rose on her toes and as I made my way she waved again then she faded and the image dissolved.

Two forty-five in the afternoon, but what afternoon, what day and where was I? It seemed good to have my watch. I decided to name myself. I'm not sure why, but it seemed a logical thing and it tended to fill the void that surrounded me. I called myself Jonathan and immediately I felt less alone. Jonathan, for some reason I couldn't capture, felt comfortable, but I didn't believe I was Jonathan. That is the beginning as best as I can tell it.

2

◊

Jonathan searched out a flat rock and emptied his pockets studying each item as he arranged them like a surgeon preparing for an operation. The Chap Stick, though good to have otherwise did not seem too useful, the knife could be handy, but the nickel and three pennies didn't bring anything to mind. Jonathan looked at his watch and unbuckled it from his wrist. Turning it in his hand he looked off into the forest and back at the watch. Deep from somewhere in a part of his mind he began to recall how a watch could be used in place of a compass. He pursed his lips in satisfaction content that he had possibly found a small part of himself.

What I know and what I don't know, what I have and what I don't have pretty much tells me what I need. Jonathan stood comforted in the fact that if nothing more he seemed to be calm and thinking rationally. He gained confidence as his mind sorted and worked through his situation. But deep inside he felt rumblings like mini volcanos ready to pour forth the molting lava of fear, apprehension and longing. He swallowed hard as if to hold these demons at bay. He left his bounty on the rock and began to walk in expanding concentric circles. Clearly he had been brought here, but from where and why. He looked for a trail or road but found only a small disturbance on the forest floor and broken twigs. Otherwise the ground remained undisturbed or restored. Retracing his circles he returned to the rock and sat down with his legs Buddha-crossed. He rested his hands on his knee and then took several deep breaths and released them slowly, then closed his eyes. He sat quietly and listened for everything and anything that could provide direction and focus. Again, it seemed to be something learned from what seemed far away and long ago.

He sat on the forest floor, a soft carpet of yearly fallen pine needles and whatever air moved stayed high in the branches. In the multi-green shades of daylight a cacophony of forest sounds filtered down. In the passing minutes the sounds of small critters scampering through overhead branches mixed with other sounds filtering from some distance, to his right a rhythmic, intermittent sound that he could not identify, the breeze when quiet, revealed something equally distant and open, a field or pasture. He pivoted in the needles, turned his head to follow one toward the other. Like an owl hunting in the night, he honed in on the sounds then opened his eyes and stared. At first he saw only dense forest with large pine trunks bare to many feet off the ground until gradually in the distance the light appeared different, less green, and brighter. Jonathan gathered his things and stowed them away. He aligned his watch with the hour hand pointing toward the sun and then marked an invisible line half way between it and the 12. That will be south. The sound came from the south west. Jonathan strapped the watch onto his wrist and began to walk. Merging shades of green surrendered gradually from the canopy above and gave way to a brighter noontime sun. Windfalls repeatedly altered his course and he checked his watch for direction until in the distance the forest opened into a lush green meadow with a tree line of hardwoods far on the other side. Directly ahead, but still out of sight, water flowed and gurgled over and around rocks. This, Jonathan thought, must be good because water and civilization usually come together. Half way across the meadow Jonathan saw where the grass had been trampled and he kneeled to check for sign of deer, but saw only the crushed grass. He followed it until near the river's edge, tracks from a vehicle began to show in patches of soft dirt and to the west he saw what looked like an old logging road. When he got closer he could see on one side where a vehicle had backed in to turn around and its wheels had spun sod into the underbrush.

He moved through the hardwoods and down a gentle slope to a small flat area along the river. The water rushed in a symphony of sounds navigating around, through, and over rocks smoothed by years of spring melt. Jonathan kneeled and cupped his hands in the cold water. First he splashed his face and instinctively reached to remove his hat, but he wore no hat. He looked into a still pool caught behind a tree's submerged roots and studied the face he saw.

In his reflection he saw the angst and again felt the pangs of the small volcanos waiting to erupt deep inside him. He splashed his face again and sat back on the riverbank. Jonathan looked at his watch, it was three thirty. He cupped more water and let it drip down into the front of his shirt. The afternoon had turned hot, hotter than what it had seemed under the pines, and with the day waning, his hunger grew. He had no idea when he had eaten or where he was going. Climbing back up the slope, Jonathan followed his shadow to the edge of the hardwoods and headed down the logging road. It pleased him that both the road and the river headed in the same direction. The road meandered and the river followed and under any other circumstance he would have enjoyed the hike. "Lara would like this one," he thought and stopped abruptly. "Who is Lara?" Jonathan looked at his ring finger and the white band where a ring must have been. "Lara," he whispered. He tried to remember more, but in his mind doors slammed shut. Jonathan followed the road until ahead he saw a cable stretched between two posts one tipped as if loose or broken. As he got closer he could see where the cable had been cut and a short, frayed length dangled with a lock attached from a large eye bolt. A wire coat hanger had been bent and twisted to hold the cable in place. Tire tracks continued up a slight gravel bank where the edge had crumbled from tires chewing their way up the shoulder onto a paved road leaving tell-tale rubber marks as they gained purchase. Thick brush surrounded each post and Jonathan scrambled under the cable and climbed to the road's edge. In one direction the road ran straight and endless as far as he could see, and in the other it fed from a long gentle curve lined on one side by tall hardwood and on the other by ledge out cropping. He aligned his watch and determined the road ran dead north. North to where? In the distance, a deep throated rumbling came from beyond the curve. Jonathan stepped back down the slope and squatted in the grass. As the rumble shook the ground, he peered up over the shoulder and in a few minutes an oversized blue truck with blurred markings on the door thumped by with large orange cones dangling from posts on the rear and a yellow flashing light spinning on top of the cab. He stood and watched as waves of mirage rising from the hot black road absorbed the truck and finally the swirling yellow light faded.

Jonathan let himself fall backwards settling in the tall grass. He sat with his elbows resting on his knees and his face in his hands wondering if he should have waved the driver down. What and tell him "Hi, I'm Jonathan, well not really, I haven't a damn clue who I am, where I am or how I got here." If the driver didn't speed off, certain he had encountered an escapee from some loony bin; he'd probably drop me at the nearest police station. That, Jonathan decided on the one hand, could pretty much end his finding anything out on his own, but on the other hand if anyone was looking for him it might let them know; a gamble to say the least and one that ignored the why and who of how he got into this damn situation in the first place. What if whoever dumped him in the woods wants to finish what they started? He could no longer suppress the small volcanos and they erupted to the surface. First he began to sweat and then his eyes teared up and he began to tremble. He sat this way until gradually he calmed and pulled his shirt loose and wiped his face. Surely he can't be far from home and someone must be looking for him. Again he looked at his finger and tried to bring Lara to mind.

North on the opposite side of the road a sign hung from a tree and Jonathan wiped his glasses with his shirt and then scrambled up the embankment and crossed the road to see what it said. The sign hung from hammered wrought iron hooks and had a green border with the name Haskell printed in dark green block letters. The gravel road in from the paved highway had been recently graded. From the signpost, he could see nothing except a tree line on one side and a drainage ditch on the other. With no gate or fence to suggest he shouldn't, Jonathan made his way down the drive. He rounded a slight curve and passed by a low wet area with cat o' nine tails, buttercups and other wild flowers, and came within sight of a small cabin with its back tucked into the trees. A small porch sat one step up from the moss and lichen covered ledge that made up the front portion of whatever foundation existed. To one side, a yellow Old Town canoe rested, lashed to two saw horses and a long woodpile covered-top-only with a brown tarp ran alongside it. Shutters covered the front windows and boards secured them lying in a yoke at each side. The solid front door hung behind a green screen door detailed with three small pine trees carved into it. A twist lock secured the screen door and the inner door had a large hasp and lock covered with a flap of rubber. At one side of the door a wood box backed up under the shuttered window and at the other side two rocking chairs sat in waiting, though securely attached to the cabin with a chain and hook on each. Jonathan sat in the second chair and rocked for a minute. He felt a sense of warmth and familiarity and turning to look again at the yellow canoe, the log pile and the roadway, he tried but couldn't bring anything into focus. Everything fluttered by in a blurred motion like when the film goes bad in a movie theatre. Jonathan went to one of the windows and slid one of the boards out of the yokes that secured the shutters and swung each back. He peered through the window at a cabin as neat inside as it was on the outside. The windows, six over six had glazing compound holding each pane in place. Jonathan looked at his watch and then to the sky now rapidly surrendering itself to the afternoon. Large cumulus clouds that had hung low were growing in height and rolling across the sky and the changing air brought a coolness that chilled him. The cabin offered shelter and maybe food. Jonathan took his Gerber knife from his pocket and opened it. He didn't want to break a window, or anything for that matter. He carefully dug the putty out until little retainers holding the glass were revealed and these he removed one by one and stuck them in the putty of the adjacent pane. Using a penny from his pocket rather than the knife tip, which he feared would chip or break the edge, he pried the glass left and right from the wood frame until it came free. With the pane of glass set against the cabin wall, he reached in until he could unlatch the window's lock. The window slid up with little resistance and Jonathan hooked one leg over the sill and then pivoted his back under the sash then pulled his other leg through taking care not to damage anything or further violate the cabin's owners. Jonathan found a pad of paper with an advertisement from a drug company and an earthen vase with pencils. He looked through papers and pamphlets on a side table hoping to find something with an address, anything that might reveal where he was, but he found nothing. Jonathan sat at the pine table in the center of the cabin's kitchen, looked around for a minute and then wrote:

*Dear Friends,*

*I apologize for entering your cabin, but let me explain my situation in hopes you will understand. I have found myself in the middle of these woods not knowing how I got here or even who I am. I am calling myself Jonathan if for no other reason than to feel that I am someone. It is getting late in the afternoon and I need shelter, some food and water. I have borrowed some items that I have listed below and will return with them and or payment for them.*

*I took great care to enter without causing damage. I will replace the glass pane I removed, but you will need to re-glaze it.*

*I am sorry to have violated your space and hope that you can understand.*

*Jonathan*

Jonathan set the note in the middle of the table and placed a small plate on the corner. Then he spotted a green spiral notebook on the table next to the vase of pencils. One page had a list with each item crossed off. Jonathan tore this page out and set it next to the pencil vase. Back at the table he took the note and added: *Also borrowed the green spiral notebook and several pencils.*

The refrigerator door had been braced ajar by a chunk of cord wood on the floor, but inside Jonathan found three gallon jugs of bottled spring water, a can of coffee, and an opened box of Arm and Hammer baking soda. He took one gallon jug of water and set it on the drain board next to the sink. The cabinets were well stocked with canned goods, from baked beans to Raviolis to brown bread, and even several cans of Spam. Jonathan took a can of raviolis, two cans of beans, and one brown bread and set them next to the water. On pegs hanging next to a locked back door, Jonathan found a small day pack, water bottles, two walking sticks and a number of baseball hats and two other brimmed hats floppy and worn from years of use. An assortment of flannel shirts, a wool jacket, several choices of rain gear, and a tattered fleece hung on a free standing coat rack. He took the small pack, a water bottle, the fleece, and one of the baseball hats, but then exchanged it for one of the floppy brimmed hats. At least I'll look like I belong out here instead of like an escapee from who knows where. He turned back and slipped one of the walking sticks from its peg as well.

After a meal fashioned from the canned goods he found, Jonathan defeated his hunger but as the curtains closed on a disturbing day the demons inside continued to boil. With a fleece blanket he found over the back of a chair, he curled up on the couch and tried to sleep. He didn't think he had fallen asleep but woke in a start, tangled in the blanket and fighting to break free. He sat up, chilled by his sweat soaked shirt, and wrapped the blanket around his shoulders. Outside the remnants of the evening's shower made echoing plop sounds as drops fell from the trees onto the covered wood and upturned canoe. Jonathon trembled and tried to shake free of the dream that had woken him. Faces were swirling in front of him, the mouths gaping and moving like goldfish in a fish bowl but they made no sound and then they merged into each other until a single mouth opened and closed as if speaking or crying or gasping. In the haze of his dream, something pulled him backward and a curtain fell across his face and all went dark. As he sat there rocking back and forth, the small volcanos inside erupted and the molting lava of fear and longing burst forth trampling his attempts to stay calm. He didn't know who he was or where he was but he did know that calm would prevail over panic. Jonathan rose from the couch taking the green fleece with him and went to where he had left out a jug of bottled water. At the sink he drank from the jug and then stripped off his wet shirt and washed his face. He took the tattered fleece from the pegs in back and hung his shirt over the chair to dry. Back on the couch he took several deep breaths and pulled the blanket up under his chin. His fists clenched the blanket tight to his neck and he tried to remember anything. He closed his eyes and in the darkness images spun by in rapid fire motion dissolving into each other, but never becoming clear or meaningful. The depth of aloneness compounded with not knowing left him trembling. He pulled the fleece closer and after much tossing and turning, sleep conquered his pain and fear.

◊

"Well ma'am, the 24 hour waiting period is actually somewhat of a myth." The police chief spoke in a soft but firm tone. "If the circumstances surrounding a missing person are suspicious, unusual or linked to some violence then we want to deal with the issue immediately. Please, have a seat." The Chief gestured toward an arm chair positioned in front of a large desk. Her blue gray uniform with silver accents and a wide black belt, though draped in masculinity, failed to conceal the lean trim figure of a young woman very much in charge of herself and the moment. The newspaper article that ran the story of Anne Vaillancourt's appointment noted how few woman chiefs there actually were. Anne Vaillancourt sat down behind the desk and rolled her chair forward. Her shoulder length brown hair, pulled back and clipped with a large tortoise shell barrette and her brown eyes, warm and comforting gathered Lara in.

"Mrs. Anderson? It is Mrs.?"

"Yes, Lara Anderson." Lara sat with her hands clasped tightly together and resting in her lap.

"Lara, before we go too far I need to point out that there are a number of reasons that can make a person appear to be

13

missing and many of them don't require law enforcement to be involved. I don't mean to be insensitive, but scenarios such as another relationship, financial problems, and medical issues are a few to be considered. Is there anything you want to tell me before we begin?"

"I'm certain none of those have anything to do with Patrick missing." Lara tried to relax, but couldn't stop her foot from tapping on the wide pine floor and her hands from strangling each other. "I'm sure every wife must say the same thing."

Anne raised her eyebrows and smiled gently. "Let's start at the beginning. When did you decide your husband was missing?"

"When he didn't come back from his morning walk. We were packed and planned to leave at ten."

"It's only two now. Could he have been delayed or run into a friend?"

"Patrick makes the coffee every morning at five and I join him on the porch at 5:30. A little after six he'll go outside and usually for his walk. He's always back at the cabin in two hours or less and this morning I reminded him we had to leave by ten, and he called back, "I'll make it short." She'd said the same thing to herself over and over since eight that morning, annoyed and angry at first, then worried.

"It's his quick hike along the tree line overlooking Turtle Pond. He never runs into anyone at that time of the morning." Anne jotted down notes as Lara spoke and waited for her to continue. "Another trail, not used much, comes in from the road. It's short and he'd only use it when he planned to hike around the pond."

"Did you go out and look for him or call for him?" Anne asked, tapping her pencil end to end on her desk.

"Yes, but only as far as the large flat rock where he sits to read and where we sometimes have picnics."

"You bought the old Wilson camp didn't you?"

"We did, an old hunting camp back in the day we have been told. It's been a project, but Patrick made it quite nice." Lara managed a slight smile.

"Your access road is the long dirt road quite a ways down from the trail from your picnic rock?"

"It is. That's what attracted Patrick when we bought the cabin."

"That trail from your picnic rock out to the road is pretty much over grown, almost abandoned. I've been down it part way. I think I recall a land dispute, maybe even before the Wilson's." Anne leaned forward in her chair and let the pencil roll across the desk. With her hands on the desk she stood up.

"I'll take a ride out to the old trail head, Lara. For now, it will be helpful if you'd make a list of exactly what your husband was wearing, what he had with him and anything else that comes to mind. Can you stay at the cabin for today? I doubt you have cell coverage there so I'll swing by later."

"The only cell coverage is at a spot on the road where the pines aren't too tall, but otherwise only at the picnic rock. I'll wait at the cabin."

15

Anne Vaillancourt handed Lara a yellow legal pad and a pencil. "I'll be right back." She touched Lara's shoulder as she went into the front office. Lara could hear her make a phone call, but she returned quickly. Lara slid the pad onto the desk and stood up.

The list was short and Lara handed it to Anne. "

"Patrick had beige shorts on, a blue tech wick T-shirt, and his leather hiking boots. He had his watch on, his glasses, and he carried his walking stick. He always wears his hat, a soft crushable fedora with a brown band. I didn't find his cell phone at the cabin so he must have taken it. He often checked the home answering machine from the rock."

Anne set the pad on her desk and thanked Lara, then walked her to the door. "I'll stop by your cabin as soon as I have had a chance to take a look." Lara looked back before getting into her Explorer and Anne smiled and waved.

It struck Anne, that although upset, Lara Andersen did not seem as unraveled as one might expect. Maybe she is just a very controlled woman. Her call to the deputy while Lara made the list might provide additional background on the Andersens.

## CHAPTER TWO
### *Pine Creek Township*

Anne Vaillancourt, like her two older brothers, one older sister, and just about everyone else, left Pine Creek right after high school. Pine Creek wasn't even a town, merely a township that depended on surrounding towns, the county and the state for most everything. More often than not a place you left and probably didn't come back to, a hunting and fishing destination at best and even that damn near dried up when the interstate decided they'd cut right through it. But unlike her brothers and sister, Anne had a plan; she knew what she wanted and had every intention of coming back. The two things Pine Creek did have were its own police department and dump and Anne intended to be its first full time Chief of police, following in her dad's footsteps. After college, with degree in hand, she enrolled in the police academy, passed up positions with the Maine State Police, and returned to Pine Creek to have her own father pin his badge on her. Only then did she succumb to the never ending courting by her longtime and loyal hometown boyfriend, Clint, married and a year later had their own little girl.

Anne eased her super-sized Ford pick-up, with sassy gold lettering and all the requisite lighting, off the edge of the road where the old trailhead was barely visible. A weathered and broken post clung to the remnants of a faded brown sign that dangled from a rusted nail. She slipped the radio's hand set from the yoke on the dash and keyed into the station to advise her deputy, Dick Flanagan, that she was leaving her vehicle. She and Dick were the extent of law enforcement for miles in all directions, with the warden service overlapping. Truckers knew this stretch of highway well as did locals and some seasonal people, but otherwise it's a long and lonesome stretch not unlike the Haynesville Woods made famous by Dick Curless.

As expected, the overgrown trailhead appeared abandoned except for a broken branch larger than what an animal might break and at first glance appeared untouched. Anne touched and smelled a small maple branch that appeared to be a recent break. Parting this branch and several more, she stepped onto the trail. Ahead, the ground, a trampled salad of small wild flowers and toppled toadstools, and gouges on the trail suggested something had been dragged. Winding around a large boulder, the trail unfolded into a small heath within sight of the "picnic rock." The grass, beaten into the dirt hid all foot prints except for several in the exposed dirt. Anne kneeled and brushed the prints with a small pine bough until three different prints were revealed. She raked through the crushed grass in concentric circles toward the heath's edge. She found very little: a partly disintegrated gum wrapper, a squashed can possibly beer or soda, two condom wrappers and a soiled and faded handkerchief with a wreath like pattern of small pink roses. As she swept the stick back toward the center the stick clicked against something and from the bent grass she uncovered a black plastic clip that may have been used to hold a cell phone. The clip was clean and unbroken. From her pant pocket she brought out a Ziploc bag and using her pen she caught the clip under its spring and carefully dropped it into the bag and then retraced her circles looking for a phone.

At the picnic rock Anne stepped up onto the smooth top and stood looking first toward Turtle Pond, imagining how Patrick Anderson might have sat, then back toward the heath then toward the Andersen camp. Aside from one print at the base of the rock in gravel that accumulated from winters of weathering of the rock, all was undisturbed.

The road could be seen from the rock, but only by someone knowing where to look and even then the boulder would block any clear view. Walking back toward her vehicle, Anne scanned the trail side for anything. She leaned back against the heavy steel push bar attached to the front of her pick-up and folded her arms across her chest and studied the road in front and back. She leaned forward and stepped away from the truck when something on the opposite side caught her eye. She looked both ways, but this road saw infrequent and intermittent traffic. The regular run through by UPS and Fed Ex shared the road with the truckers leaving the road a long lonesome highway otherwise.

Caught in the branch of a wild thorny bush, a matchbook sized scrap of yellow cloth fluttered in the breeze and below a scuffle of foot prints and similar drag marks. At the height of the road's shoulder, crushed grass had given way to marks in the sod which pulverized the lupine along the edge. Tangled in the crushed flowers she found two narrow strips of paper neatly folded in half. Using her pen Anne poked at them and raked them free of the grass and unfolded them. One a credit card receipt from Perry's hardware store with a date and time stamp and the other a receipt for cash from "—rt's deli," with the top corner missing. Both appeared to have been folded to fit into a man's wallet and Anne searched the brush, but did not find a wallet.

◊

Lara arrived back at the cabin, turned the vehicle off and sat with her arms wrapped around the steering wheel and for the first time felt the worry that had been with her all morning begin to drown her. She rested her forehead on the steering wheel and allowed herself to cry. Patrick and Lara were similar in many ways from the very beginning. They were both "get-er-done type personalities." If something can be done, do it, they believed, otherwise move on. Lara sat up and shook the steering wheel. "I'm doing all I can," she cried out to the car, the cabin, the trees and whoever and whatever else might be listening. She got out of the car and slammed the door as if somehow it was to blame. The Explorer, innocent of any blame, sparkled in the diffused light that sliced through the pine boughs. Had it not been for a model redesign its ten years wouldn't't even be noticeable. Patrick was as particular about his Explorer as he was about everything. "Take care of what you have or you won't have anything," he would say.

With the children grown, educated and, for the most part, tucked into their own lives, Lara and Patrick decided to slow down, and part of slowing down had been the cabin, a little gift to themselves they had often talked about but nothing more. Patrick never really discussed retiring, as much as redirecting and refocusing. He wasn't a man content to settle for gaining too much weight, wasting too much time and taking too many naps. The cabin was a steal as far as Maine real estate goes, virtually abandoned and left to the ravages of nature when old man Wilson died. Apparently the daughter had left the area and the son going through his second divorce cared only about whatever money he could get out of the old camp. A bit more of a fixer upper than Lara had anticipated, or even agreed to for that matter, but as the weekends piled one on another, each trip seemed like a new honeymoon. "So much for slowing down after sixty," Patrick joked one afternoon when he and Lara were setting a new carrying beam overhead to support a cantilevered loft to house a guest bed, a rug each side and nothing more. "Just enough, but not too much." Lara slapped Patrick on the back as she passed him. "We don't want company turning into three day old fish." You had to drive twenty-eight miles to any type of grocery store and eighteen to Mack's which had gas (most of the time) and some essentials; so if you wanted it and thought you needed it, you better have brought it with you. The police station / post office / fire truck garage, all sat half way between Mack's and the grocery store, which had a faded and chipped IGA sign, but otherwise no discernible name. Everyone knew Mack Bridges, the owner, and Mack's stuck as the name of choice.

◊

Lara stood for a while and looked out from the small porch and then went inside, dropped into Patrick's stuffed chair and crossed her ankles on the ottoman. The cabin had been cleaned from corner to corner; everything ready for them to leave. "A place for everything and everything in its place." Patrick almost sang this as his personal song, but gave the Shakers due credit when forced.

Lara thought about her daughters and wondered when she should tell them. Is it too early? Lucinda and Lynn were as different as daughters could be. Both independent and capable young women, but each charged in from a different direction. Lara almost dreaded Lynn's advance into a situation, more often than not a bit critical whereas Lucinda came in as the organizer and officer in charge a get-er-done personality like her father. Lara became more concerned and even frightened as the hours peeled away, but she could do nothing more now but wait, wait for Patrick's footsteps on the porch, but Anne Vaillancourt's crunching tires came next.

Before Anne could turn off the engine, Lara came out the door and down the steps to the porch. Anne stepped from the truck, buttoning the pocket flap on her shirt and walked toward Lara leaving the door to her truck open. Not knowing what to say, Lara opened the screen door to the cabin and swung her open hand in a welcoming gesture. "We haven't really opened it for the season yet."

Anne quickly saw that Lara's anxiety had ratcheted up. Her obvious waiting at the door and tightness in her face replaced the softer and gentler demeanor of earlier.

"Impressive." Anne said, in an attempt to relax the moment. She turned in a small circle and looked up at the small loft.

"I visited a long time ago, not Chief then. The Wilson girls and I went to school together. They had a party of sorts here after graduation—you're right about you and your husband making it comfortable." Anne looked toward the small overstuffed couch.

"Please, have a seat." Lara sat in Patrick's chair, on the edge as if waiting for a timer to go off or a baby to cry from its crib.

"I found a few things, they might help us and they might not," Anne settled back into the couch reaching to move a pillow to one side. "There is no question that something happened out beyond your picnic rock, but I'm not sure what." "Did you and your husband go to Perry's Hardware on your way to the cabin?"

"Perry's Hardware?" Lara sat back and then righted herself back on the edge. "Yes, actually Patrick went over. He dropped me at Bart's Deli to pick up sandwiches. He had to get a part for something. I can't remember what. Why?"

The chief leaned forward and laid the Ziploc bag with the two receipts she found on the table and carefully smoothed the plastic over them. "I found these in the underbrush on the other side of the rock. Lara picked up the bag with the receipts. "These should have been in his wallet." Lara looked up at Anne. "I had given him the one from Bart's. He logs all expenses in a journal on his lap top. Was..."

"No, I didn't find his wallet, but I found this," Anne laid the phone clip on the table. "Is this your husband's?"

"Yes." Lara leaned forward with her arms resting on her knees and wrung her hands as if massaging in hand cream and then brought them up pressing her mouth onto her clenched fists.

"Some sort of scuffle took place out there and tracks suggested a vehicle left the side of the road." Anne decided not to mention the scrap of cloth yet. She wanted to wait and see what else was found. "My deputy headed out there and I want to walk in from this end. I want to do a more thorough sweep, take some pictures. I don't mean to be alarming but it appears your husband may have met up with someone in what does not appear to be a friendly encounter. Anne stood up and gathered things from the table. "Do you and your husband carry the same credit cards?"

"We carry two that are the same and I have a third that I carry."

"Okay, take the two that match your husbands and don't use them. Give me those numbers so I can put a trace on them. Whoever has his wallet may try to use his credit cards. Can you think of anything else?"

"No, I guess his medical card, his license. Patrick hated a fat wallet and carried very little. He didn't even carry much cash."

"ATM card?"

"I don't know." Lara slid off the edge of her chair, stood up and faced Anne. "

What have they done to Patrick? Why? Was there–do you think he is okay. He walks there all the time. How can this happen? Do you think he's okay?" Lara stepped toward Anne as if to emphasize her questions and then brought her hands to her face and slowly shook her head.

"I do. No serious sign of violence appeared a scuffle of some kind, but nothing more. We don't have much to go on, but I believe someone has him for some reason."

Lara got up and started toward the kitchen, turned back and then started again. "What should I do?"

"It's probably best you go home, stay near a phone and try to remain calm. Is there someone who can come be with you?" Anne Vaillancourt stepped toward Lara and placed her hand on her shoulder. "I'm going to walk in from this end and meet Deputy Flanagan. Give me a number where I'll be able to reach you."

"I'll be okay, I'll drive home. One of our girls will come over." Lara straightened her back and squared her shoulders as if to do battle. "I'll be fine."

Lara walked with Anne to the porch and watched as she backed the big Ford truck around. As Anne headed down the driveway, she looked back at the cabin and Lara had gone in. Anne thought back to the party graduation night at the then Wilson cabin; a life time ago it seemed now. A tame party as far as graduation parties go, but Anne remembered when Tammy Wilson's brother and a couple other guys came crashing into the festivities. Literally crashing in that they took out one of the porch supports when they cut the turn too close with their rusted out, wired together Ford Maverick. To say they'd been drinking would be an understatement. It was like playing dodge ball once they got inside. They were all hands and keeping them off you was like swatting flies, big nasty smelling, beer-gutted flies. In the end it all turned out fine. Somehow, no one really knew how, but they were convinced to leave before anything too physical became part of the grab-assing. Clint Vaillancourt and Tammy took one of them aside and said something that restored order. Through all their years together and several years of marriage, Clint never told Anne what was said. He just smiled, but when she became Chief everything came clear.

◊

Lara called Lucinda, the younger of their two daughters, as soon as she had cell coverage. She pulled over when Lucy answered and shut off the car. Taking a deep breath and trying to stay calm like Anne Vaillancourt had instructed, she slowly told Lucy what had happened. Lynn, their older daughter was in Boothbay to meet up with Lynn's daughter, who arrived that afternoon returning from a two month sail aboard one of those "get to know yourself and your fellow man" educational cruises. Lucy insisted that her mother not drive home. She told Lara to get to Lincoln and rent a room and call as soon as she was settled.

"Drive carefully; I'm on my way, Mom. What phone did you give the police chief?"

"My cell phone."

"Great. Wait for her call and tell her I'm on my way."

# CHAPTER THREE
*Greta's Golden Grub*

Jonathan got up early to a morning clearing and surrendering itself to the natural sounds of the forest with only lingering drops falling as the leaves warmed. He shook off the last of sleep's haze and the undefinable remnants of final dreams and sat for a moment on the edge of the couch, quickly recognizing the cabin. He did not know who he was or how this all happened to him, but still there were certain innate parts of one's character that rise to the call and prevail. Jonathan knew in spite of his anxiety, apprehension and shadows of fear, control not panic must prevail. It is part of the human character to accept routine as a norm even the most disturbing routines. Still, he listened carefully for any sound and then walked from window to window and from a position hidden to the side, looked out scanning the tree line and surrounding area. Having stopped not far from where he found himself, certainly anyone looking or following would come to this Haskell cabin. And of course, the owners could arrive at any time. He opened the door and looked out and listened more then stepped out. Convinced all was quiet and safe he went back inside.

Jonathan straightened the couch where he had slept then refolded the green fleece blanket and positioned it back across one arm where he found it. He took a camp style percolator from the cabinet under the sink and using water from one of the jugs of Poland Spring water he made coffee and settled for spam and some dried crackers for breakfast.

With everything put back in proper order he made his way outside where he fitted the pane of glass back into its frame and using his knife he pressed the small metal points into place. He folded the shutters closed and placed the bar across them. The overnight rain left the morning cool and he put the fleece on and positioned the hat on his head. It fit well and this pleased him. With water bottle, food and a borrowed thermos filled with the remaining coffee, Jonathan headed down the drive to the highway. He walked briskly revisiting his thoughts of the night before. In his mind they were a neat outline: I've got to have a plan, some kind of story, something believable. He reassured himself that someone must be missing him. Clearly I belong somewhere. He thought about going to the police, but wasn't sure yet what he might say. For now, taking care not to reveal himself to whoever did this, he planned to find out. Some early birds on the driveway's edge joined the morning's quiet and Jonathan's thoughts.

At the highway Jonathan looked both ways. Crossing the road didn't seem necessary, so Jonathan turned right and headed north. With a plan of sorts and feeling a little more in control, Jonathan felt good and rubbed the stubble on his face and wished he had shaved. The highway ran straight as far as he could see and in a short while a dark burgundy trailer truck came from the north. As it passed, Jonathan read *Hannaford* on the side. "Hannaford," he thought. For a second it sounded familiar, but it was fleeting. He looked at his watch and noted that it was 6:20 when the Hannaford truck passed heading south. A half hour passed before he heard the sound of another truck, this one came from the south. Jonathan turned and faced the coming truck and held out his thumb. He could hear the truck begin to slow from some distance away and as it neared Jonathan it continued past and rolled to a stop.

Jonathan turned and ran toward the stopped truck. The truck glistened as though it were brand new. The cab, a deep forest green had gold letters on the door: *"Stillman Transport"* and under that *Houlton, Maine.* Jonathan grabbed the big chrome assist bar and stepped up and opened the door. The driver, a small man, almost dwarfed by the size of his truck's cab, smiled across at Jonathan. He wore khaki pants and a yellow shirt with button down pocket flaps. A pair of sunglasses dangled on a cord around his neck and his hair, brown and wavy, was combed as if he had just come from church.

31

"Morning, friend, hop aboard." The driver extended a hand as Jonathan settled into the seat and reached for a seat belt. "Brad Stillman and you are?"

"Jonathan, Jonathan Ford," Jonathan said quickly remembering the Hanna*ford* truck that went by.

There was a loud hiss as the air brakes relieved themselves and Brad Stillman directed the truck back onto the highway. A lot of shifting and soon the truck reached a speed which seemed to settle at about eighty.

"So, where you headed, Jonathan Ford?"

Comforted by the sound of another voice, Jonathan felt layers of his concerns peel off like the skin of an onion. He looked across the wide console at Brad Stillman and smiled. "Headed, that damn road is so lonely you almost forget where you're headed or even where you came from. Hell you can damn near forget who you are out there."

"A lot's been said about this stretch of highway and I think you may have summed it up." Brad smiled and shook his head. "Houlton is where I'm headed. Got a good return load waiting north of there. Just delivered a load coming up from Raleigh, North Carolina to Bangor."

Jonathan shifted in his seat and under his knees he repositioned his pack against the seats front. Tucked between the center console and the seat a folded paper stuck up. "Is that today's paper?"

"No, yesterday's Portland Press Herald." The driver reached behind the console and retrieved another paper. "Here, this morning's Bangor Daily News, fresh off the press. Jonathan took the paper and read the top header: *Bangor, Maine May 18, 2012.* Again something seemed familiar, but it dissipated like a small puff of smoke. Jonathan opened the paper and scanned the pages for anything he might recognize. He looked for a story on a missing person or anything else that might suggest his being missing. Politics, economics and pretty much a mixture of life in Maine played out across each page. Maybe it takes longer for a missing person to be news. Well, at the least, he knew he was in Maine!

Brad looked down at Jonathan's pack, his stick and then up at him. "Hiking, camping?"

"A little of both, trying to stay away from the camping part, but seems to be quite a bit of hiking, got a bit of a project going." Jonathan pulled on the belt that crossed his chest and turned slightly in the seat. Another big truck passed by heading south and the truck rocked slightly.

"I'm writing a story, sort of a documentary about travelling lonesome highways. It's supposed to be a minimalistic venture with no money and few supplies. The intent is to see how far you can successfully make it on the highway working as need be as you go and finding shelter where you can. I pitched the idea to a couple of magazines and got some bites."

The driver downshifted as they approached a curve. "You're kidding. You mean to tell me you're headed north on this road, not knowing where you will sleep next and you don't have any money?"

"Got a dime, a nickel and three pennies" Jonathan smiled. "Like I said, I've been so broke and lonely I've almost forgotten who I am." Jonathan thought back to how he laid this out in his head the night before and thought it almost sounded believable, a little strange , but believable.

"Damn crazy if you ask me." The driver shook his head.

"Sure is and you just became a character in my story. Mind if I use your name?"

Brad Stillman gives Jonathan a thumbs up. "Be my guest." The morning sun filtered down on the highway and once in a while a car or pickup passed heading south, to Bangor Jonathan assumed. "Tell you what, there's a good stop a ways ahead. I'll buy you a coffee and breakfast too if you'd like."

"I'd like that very much."

Brad Stillman pulled the big truck off the highway into a gravel parking lot where an assortment of vehicles had parked helter-skelter with no sense of order. Drivers left some running and others they shut down. The restaurant, if you want to call it that, consisted of an eclectic combination of an old stainless steel diner, a small trailer and a wood addition on the south west. Booths lined each side as you entered. All had red vinyl seats and white Formica tops wrapped on the edge with ribbed stainless steel. Along a counter, red and chrome swivel stools were all taken. On the counter an array of tiered covered plates displayed an assortment of doughnuts, cake slices, pie wedges, and cookies. Two attractive girls wearing cut off blue jeans and tee shirts that said *Greta's Golden Grub* and aprons tied around their waists moved to and fro behind the counter. At the end of the counter as you entered, a gentleman with a soiled baseball hat and a beard that touched the counters edge sat tapping his spoon on the edge of his mug. He mumbled something or maybe sang under his breath. It seemed rhythmic and he repeated it continuously. Others, along the counter seemed to know each other or otherwise engaged in shared conversations. Someone at some time had a serious fondness for Ford's. The wall high above the window that looked into the kitchen had been covered with Ford emblems and other items that stretched from one end to the other and even onto the ceiling. A woman who appeared to be about seventy worked beyond a window connecting to the kitchen. Her hair, tucked into a net, had a pencil stuck through the net and into it and a faded Boston Red Sox Jersey hung cinched at her waist by a well-used apron. In the rear section shelves lining each wall displayed everything from toothbrushes to shaving kits, to bibles to replacement radio cords.

Several people greeted Brad, and Greta waved from the kitchen "Up for the weekend or passing through?" she hollered through the window as we made our way to a booth.

"Headed to Kitty's to spend some time with the grand-kids. Quick turn-around. Got a load going back to Bangor." Brad waved and continued to the booth and one of the girls followed.

Brad and Jonathan slid into a booth at the far end where the supply store met the diner. Brad took two menus from behind a salt and pepper caddy that held two moose headed shakers and handed one to Jonathan.

"Morning Brad, good to see you." The young waitress set two white mugs on the table, poured the coffee, and then stood with pad in hand snapping her gum. She looked young and Jonathan wondered why she wasn't in school. "Something different today or your regular?"

"Regular is good, thanks, how about you Jonathan?" Brad blew at the edge of his mug and then carefully sipped the coffee.

"Jonathan looked up from the menu and said "Greta's eggs, #2 sounds good. Can I have sausage instead of bacon? Do you have cranberry juice?"

"You got it," the young girl turned snapping her gum as she left.

"Thanks Brad." Jonathan rubbed the stubble on his face. "I hate it when I don't shave."

Brad slid out of the booth and walked to a rack in the center of the supply store. He returned and dropped a package that contained a razor, a small can of Gillette shaving cream, a tooth brush and a travel size Colgate tooth paste. "Here, there's a shower room around the corner, go shave." Jonathan smiled, picked up the shrink wrapped package and swung out of the booth. He shaved quickly and washed up and by the time he returned the young girl arrived with their breakfasts.

The young girl set Jonathan's breakfast down and Brad's waffles in front of him. "Cranberry juice coming, anything else?" Brad scanned the table as if taking inventory. "Nope, I think we're good to go, Thanks, Becky."

Brad filled each little pocket in his waffles with a dab of butter and then drizzled syrup over them.

"So," he said looking up as he cut the waffle with his fork. "Your little project, are you looking for work right now?"

Jonathan finished chewing the bite of egg and home fry in his mouth. "Probably a good idea. The rules, if you want to call them that, are for me to get whatever I can through the goodwill of others, barter and trade and any other way that doesn't involve stealing or breaking a law. So far it is working and I thank you again for this." Jonathan took a piece of his pumpernickel toast and broke it in half and dipped it in the egg's yolk. "I actually keep a log so I can re-pay anyone who has played a part in this venture so don't run off without giving me an address."

It intrigued Jonathan, how his little story had manifested into reality. Brad's company and hospitable demeanor had relaxed him and his concerns and worries settled deep inside him, no doubt pushed aside by the comfort of eating and human companionship. He wasn't sure what was next, but he would need to do something to support himself through this search. Miles separated him from where he found himself and no doubt from where he belonged. This adventure seemed to be writing its own rules as he moved along. Finding out who he was remained in the forefront of his mind, but he would need help along the way.

"I've got a friend; a Maliseet who lives out by the Meduxnekeag River—he raises sheep and llamas. He may want some temporary help. He's rebuilding a small barn and running some new fence line." Brad slid waffle squares around soaking up the maple syrup on his plate.

"Sheep and llamas, sounds like an odd combination."

"Not really, believe it or not the llamas protect the sheep. There isn't a dog or coyote around that'll mess with a couple of llamas coming at them. I can give him a call if you're interested."

Jonathan picked up his mug of coffee and looked over at Brad. "Very interested, thanks."

"Good, we'll drop the rig at my daughter's, you can meet the grand-kids and we'll take her pick-up out to see Togquos."

"Togquos?"

"It's Algonquin for twin. Maliseet - Passamaquoddy share the Algonquin language. Old Tog is a twin. His brother died."

They reached Brad's daughter's house, on a side road five miles off the highway, twenty five miles farther north. A well maintained, split level on a large piece of land with a couple out buildings. A fenced section stretched along one side with a long pull through of gravel tracks and sod center. A yellow ribbon encircled a tree at the driveway entrance and as Brad pulled the rig up along the fence past a pick-up truck, Jonathan saw a Marine Corps sticker on the rear window. A young German Shepard came running out not at all threatening, almost frolicking. A woman came from the front door with a toddler on her hip and another dashed from around her and ran toward Brad who had come around from in front of the truck. Jonathan stepped down from the truck and watched the scene unfold. The little boy threw himself almost flying through the air into Brad's arms and Brad swung him around in a big circle. The mother continued, reaching Brad quickly and with her free arm encircled his neck and kissed his cheek. "Hey Dad, good run?"

"Not bad, not bad at all. Hey Jonathan come meet my daughter Kitty and my grand-children, Olivia, and Daniel."

Kitty turned and smiled. "Hello Jonathan, nice to meet you." She looked at Jonathan's shorts and hiking boots and then turned back to her father.

"Bet you stopped at Greta's on the way in. Want more coffee?" Kitty shifted the little girl from one hip to the other glancing back at Jonathan.

"I think we're good, but thanks" Brad lowered Daniel to the ground but kept hold of his hand. "What do you hear from Dan?"

"Still on schedule as far as we know, 19 days and counting, but there's been a lot of bad stuff happening, so keep your fingers crossed."

"Their Daddy is in Afghanistan, but he's due home real soon now." Brad rustled the boy's hair as they turned toward the house. "Come on in."

Kitty turned to Jonathan and smiled. "Can get a bit hectic, but if you know how to dodge a couple of little rascals you'll be fine."

Inside, the toddler set free, immediately scampered toward an assortment of toys in the living room. Before Jonathan could even wonder if he had any knowledge of "dodging little rascals," Daniel came over and looked up at him, but said nothing.

Jonathan, listening to what Kitty and Brad were saying, looked down when the young boy began tapping his knee, "Mister, are you a truck driver like Buppie?"

"No, I just met your Buppie this morning. I'm a..." Jonathan paused for a second, "I write stories."

"I have stories. Do you want to read a story?"

"Sure, that sounds like fun." Daniel turned and ran into the living room and came back in no time with a bundle of books. Kitty started to get up and intervene. "It's fine." Jonathan wasn't sure where it came from, but it felt familiar and good.

Brad took his cell phone to call Togquos. "He might even have his phone turned on. Phones are one of his ongoing love/hate relationships. He needs it at times but it isn't unusual for him to keep it turned off." He walked around the house as he spoke and kneeled twice to adjust something on the intricate Lincoln Log construction on the floor. Daniel and Jonathan continued to read and Kitty attended to dishes in the sink.

Brad and Kitty needed to look at something to do with the sump pump in the basement. She picked up the little girl and looked over at Daniel and Jonathan.

"We're good." Jonathan smiled as he and Daniel started the

third story.

When Brad came up from the basement, he said, "Tog didn't answer so we'll take a ride up. No doubt he stuffed his phone in a drawer." Before Jonathan headed out to the pickup with Brad, Daniel had steered him through five stories.

# CHAPTER FOUR
### *Togquos*

By the time Brad backed the pick-up around and onto the lawn one way or another they had chewed up most of the morning. Brad pulled the pick-up onto the road and headed out. "We can get there on the highway, but this is more fun, not any quicker, but more fun." The pavement soon ended and Jonathan began to see the fun Brad meant when the road surrendered to deep ruts and mud from spring rains; at times though, even when driving through shallow washouts, it was solid packed gravel. This went on for several miles and then they rose out of it and began to see open pasture on both sides. Soon sheep began to appear and on the edge not mingling but standing like sentries, llamas kept a watchful eye. As they rounded a gentle curve an old two story house with weathered clapboards came into view tucked under a cluster of maples and oaks. In the dirt drive an old Ford Pick-up truck with an extended cab, a newer Jeep Wrangler, and a Polaris Ranger ATV sat parked in a random, haphazard pattern. Next to what might be the new barn site, a large man had a sheep turned half onto his knee and leaned over it attending to something. As our tires crunched in the gravel he looked up and let the sheep free and it hopped then wobbled and darted toward the rear of the house. The man stood from where he had been sitting on a large stump and set something down on the stump. He wore western chaps held around his waist with a length of rope. A sweat shirt with the sleeves cut or maybe torn off, hung loose. A beaded band held his long hair, neatly parted in the middle, in place. He came toward us stepping around a watering trough and he and Brad embraced slapping each other on the back. The man towered over Brad and it looked as though the repeated back slapping might knock Brad off his feet.

"Welcome." The man stood tall and straight like a telephone pole. The warm brown of his eyes gathered you in and captured you in his gaze. His grip, full and tight, but not crushing confirmed his welcome. His voice, deep and soft had a caressing and comforting tone.

"Tog, this is Jonathan." Brad stepped aside and left Jonathan facing Tog. "He might be handy on your projects." Brad added.

Tog stood back and looked him up and down. "You're looking for work?" Tog said, as he looked Jonathan over. "You look fit to me. When did you want to start?" Jonathan smiled. This guy doesn't waste any time. He looked at his watch.

"Now." Jonathan smiled and adjusted his hat.

Tog let out a hearty laugh that all of his upper body seemed to participate in. "Well, how about after I give you two some lunch." He stepped forward and wrapped his arms around each of them and directed them to the house.

Hardly twenty-four hours had passed since Jonathan found himself in the woods and already he was accepting a job. How would this impact his plan to find out what happened and who he was, a plan rapidly evolving? Clearly, he had to do something to support himself. He would figure each step as he goes. This fell short of calming the feeling that this left him drifting farther away rather than getting closer.

Six steps took you from the walk onto a farmer's porch. To the left of the entry, stood an intricately stacked pile of fire wood and to the right a large green rocker with a tattered and faded pillow with a string fringe, and on a small table next to that lay a long stemmed pipe. Tog pulled open an oversized screen door then pushed open a wooden door that unlike the weathered and faded clapboards was meticulously finished a deep walnut that accented multiple carvings. Jonathan followed Brad through the door and turned to look at the door, touching the carvings as he passed.

"Made it myself." Tog followed us in and left the door open. On the left, in a room that had probably been the dining room, tables wrapped around the outer walls. A desk chair with wheels sat in front of one and seemed ready to roll around the perimeter. On the tables, stacks of books competed with space with what at a glance appeared to be piles of maps. The room to the right had a broad winged back chair and a large ottoman that faced a fireplace and at the front a long, deep window seat with built in drawers followed the wall. An overstuffed chair with a newspaper draped over one arm and a lamp with a stretched beige cloth shade sat close to the right. A woven basket full of magazines and a few books sat half toppled beside the chair and what looked like the remnants of peanut shells encircled a bare spot on the floor. A large rug of intricate threads intermingled in a sea of bright burgundies and blues with streaks of green and yellow flashes covered the floor. A cat, not just a cat, but the biggest cat Jonathan had ever seen, lie in the middle of the rug. The cat, although curled into itself, still covered more of the rug than it didn't.

"He's a Maine Coon cat, call him Bigcat. All one word, it seemed appropriate at the time." Tog stepped into the room and scratched Bigcat's neck and the cat stretched out its front legs and curled its paws on the rug. "He's getting older, but can still take down any critter that scampers in."

The hallway ended at a kitchen, remarkably small compared to the rest of the house. A big pine trestle table claimed the center of the room. Tog pulled a chair out and looked at Jonathan and pointed to another for Brad. From a long counter, that ran the length of the back wall uninterrupted except by a large two basin sink, Tog brought a basket with several choices of bread. To the right an old rounded top Philco refrigerator clicked as the compressor tried to keep up with itself. Tog went to the refrigerator and began bringing out plates and bowls of assorted leftovers. Brad knew the drill and went to a drawer to the left of the sink and gathered up silverware. Tog handed the dishes to Jonathan.

"Milk, apple juice, beer, water?"

One dish had what looked like the remains of a ham and another had chicken legs, and a third had what appeared to be hard boiled eggs. Tog came to the table with mustard and mayonnaise. He turned and from an open shelf over the refrigerator took three tall pint glasses each sporting a different logo. In the center of the table was a napkin holder, a bowl with pears and bananas and the same salt and pepper shakers that Jonathan had seen at Greta's.

Tog went back to the refrigerator which had completed a quick shimmy and gone silent. He leaned in and brought out three bottles of Coor's light.

"What's missing? Looks adequate dig in." Tog pulled a chair out and sat down and rolled an egg around on the table to crack its shell. That must have been the dinner bell, because in no time Bigcat was sauntering into the kitchen.

Brad and Tog talked like brothers or at least men who had shared intimate parts of their lives. Each time Tog laughed his whole body joined in. Brad told Tog about Jonathan's project and Tog looked over saying nothing at first. "You're kidding right?" he said, "well, if you need a bed too that comes out of your pay." The cat apparently did not come in for food, but instead entwined itself in and out of their legs with a deep throated purr that was fitting for its size.

When lunch ended the three men restored everything to where it had been and Brad washed the few dishes used. Tog showed Jonathan a room off of the kitchen, a large room with its own bathroom.

"The front room is for everyone, but Bigcat controls what seat you might get."

Out on the porch, Tog and Brad said their good-byes and Jonathan thanked Brad for his help. Brad said he'd be back up mid-week and would check in. Jonathan asked him for an address so he could repay him as the project finished up. Brad took a card from his wallet and a pen from his shirt. He leaned on the railing and wrote on the card then handed it to Jonathan. Jonathan took the card and read what Brad had written: *Any breast Cancer Awareness Charity.* He looked over at Brad and Brad nodded and headed down the steps. Tog and Jonathan followed him to Kitty's truck and watched as he backed up and headed out.

"So," Tog said grasping Jonathan's shoulder. "What do you know about sheep and llamas?

"Not a damn thing."

"What about carpentry?"

"Probably as much or more than I have forgotten." Jonathan smiled and Tog turned and walked toward the small barn and Jonathan followed.

A cement footing had been poured and the forms were still in place. To the side and next to a pile of sand an old gas cement mixer sat with its drum turned upside down and next to that, a metal wheelbarrow balancing on one good leg and one bent leg. Otherwise there didn't seem to be any materials on site except for two by sixes laid around the perimeter next to bolts seated in the footings. Tog picked up a large pair of pliers from the stump and a plastic bottle with a needle nose end as he passed. "That lamb had a thorn or splinter of some kind. I had just removed it when you pulled in, flushed it with some peroxide. She should be fine."

Jonathan looked around and up toward a small rise where pasture land met a young growth of hardwoods. "How many sheep do you have?"

"Well, I had about 24, but I lost three or four. Found three dead, but the fourth is still missing. May be out there hurt or maybe just crawled somewhere I haven't looked and died."

"What happened to them?"

"Coyotes mostly, sometimes a dog." Tog stood with one foot up on the footing form and looked up toward the grazing sheep. "Look over there to the southeast, that's where the lamas are now—they keep an eye on the sheep. They're a social animal like the sheep so everyone seems to get along. They don't like dogs and coyotes and can be very effective with their hooves. They don't like you to touch them about the head, especially near the eyes. They're prey more often than not and their eyes are on the side of their head. A predator, like a bear, has his eyes in front. Their eyes and nose are their first defense so they get pretty nasty if you get in the way of them. Otherwise, respect their space and everyone can be friends." Tog walked over to the cement mixer and adjusted a small piece of a tarp wrapped around the motor. Jonathan walked around the footing until he came to what must be the intended front and doorway.

"This doesn't look like a very big barn." Jonathan stopped in front and looked back through the perimeter shaped with the footings. "Where do the all the sheep and the llamas go in the winter?"

There's another old barn over that knoll. It's in pretty rough shape and not really used much. The sheep and lama are happy with any kind of three sided shelter with four inches or more of hay and a water supply. As long as they can hunker down and get out of the wind or blowing snow they do pretty well. The llamas always want to see an opening, an escape route or they get real edgy. This is for the cria, the young, which need a little more protection. One section will be for supplies and feed. Come on, we'll take the Ranger out and run the property line and I'll show you the fence line we're going to replace. You good in those shorts or do you want to change?"

Jonathan glanced down at his shorts and looked back up at Tog. "I'm good."

Tog continued walking then turned, "They're all you've got, right?" Jonathan smiled and nodded.

Large white letters read "Polaris" across the ATV's tailgate.

Tog reached in and adjusted something and then turned a key. "Let 'er warm up, I'll be right back." Tog walked to the house and took the steps two at a time. In a minute he came back out and tossed a pair of denim bib coveralls to Jonathan and went around and stepped up into the driver's seat. Jonathan caught the coveralls and let them fall open. He leaned against the front fender and stepped into each leg and positioned the straps over his shoulders then stepped up and settled in the seat. "All set?" Tog smiled and put the rig into reverse. At the end of the gravel drive, Tog stopped at a small gate in the fencing. "Get that will ya?" Jonathan quickly figured out how the gate's latch worked and swung it open. Once Tog had driven through Jonathan closed the gate and let the big "U" shaped metal fall back over the adjacent post securing it in place.

Unless the terrain got too rugged, the little rig ran relatively quiet. When it worked its way through ruts and over ledge outcroppings it whined in protest. Jonathan and Tog talked above the noise as they headed out through the pasture. They passed sections of fence folded down by windfalls; other sections had suffered in heavy snow, many were old, worn and with rotted posts. Tog explained that some areas will be replaced and some repaired with new posts set. Grazing sheep seemed only mildly interested when they approached, but the llamas watched until the rig passed by.

When they completed the tour, Tog pulled through another small gate with a similar latching system and onto the road Brad and Jonathan had driven in on and continued to bounce and weave to miss numerous pot holes. Back in the yard Tog pulled the ATV over near the barn project and shut it off. It had been a long day and Jonathan could feel the hours since leaving the Haskell's cabin. "You probably want to get settled and cleaned up." Tog came around the machine. "That bed has a cover on it, but you'll need to get some sheets from the closet in the bathroom. Towels are there too." He said no more and walked toward the house and Jonathan stood for a minute then followed. Tog stopped on the porch and waited. "Later I'll be getting something going for supper, should be ready about 6:30." Tog nodded and smiled and then walked in and went into the room where Jonathan had seen the tables stacked with books and maps. Jonathan continued down the hall and into the kitchen where he gathered up his pack and stick and went through the door off the kitchen to his room.

Inside the room, a short hallway formed the back wall of the bathroom and then it opened into a spacious room with two mulled windows that faced due west. On the opposite wall a double bed with large turned legs and a carved headboard and a smaller but similar detailed footboard. To one side of the windows a large stuffed chair sat positioned to watch out the windows and a small writing table and chair sat along the wall that led to the bathroom. Jonathan rested his walking stick in the corner and set his pack in the chair. There really wasn't anything to unpack except for the canned goods, his notebook and pencils and water bottle.

Jonathan pulled back the quilted cover on the bed, folded it and set it on the small table. In the bathroom he found a full size closet door and inside floor to ceiling shelves stocked with towels, sheets and miscellaneous bathroom supplies. He took a set of sheets and tossed them onto the bed. He couldn't remember the last time he had a shower, but then he couldn't remember much of anything. He took a bar of soap from the closet and a small travel bottle of shampoo and turned on the shower. He slipped the straps of the coveralls off his shoulder and then took off the rest of his clothes. The hot shower felt good and maybe he couldn't remember the last shower, but there was no question as to whether it was time for one.

◊

The smell of Tog's cooking distracted Jonathan from notes he was writing in his green notebook. He looked at his watch, 5:45—certain Tog didn't need or want help, he continued making notes.

_May 17, 2012–found myself_

Jonathan wrote at the top of the first page and underlined it. Then he began listing everything that came to mind.

_Haskell's Cabin—Rte. 2a—first night._

_Make list of what I took_

_Rough night—bad dreams_

_Tried to conquer the fears and anxiety._

_They had me disturbed_

_May 18 Friday_

_Met Brad Stillman—trucker_

*Brad bought me breakfast at Greta's Golden Grub*

*Nice guy*

*Met Brad's daughter, Kitty and grandchildren—Daniel and Olivia*

*Met Togquos (Tog) [pronounced like TOAD but with a "G"]*

*Took him up on offer to do some repairs*

*Phew—so much, so fast*

*I'm in Maine-North of Bangor—Near Houlton*

*Tan line on my ring finger*

*The name Lara seeps into my mind but it is fleeting*

*So far pretty lucky. Met some good people, hope I'm "good people!"*

He sat for a minute and tried to bring back the faded image of the woman waving and looked back to his ring finger and whispered: "Lara?" Jonathan folded his notebook shut and set it on the corner of the bureau. He gathered up the canned goods and walked out to the kitchen.

"Wow, does that smell good." He set the canned goods on the counter to the left of the sink. "It's not much, but it's my contribution."

Tog continued stirring the chicken and vegetables, the source of the incredibly pleasing smell and looked over at Jonathan's cans. "You best keep the ravioli and beans you may need them, but the brown bread looks good. Open it up."

Jonathan's hunger was intense or Tog was a great cook, probably both, but supper brought a fine end to a long day. Tog washed dishes at the sink and Jonathan dried them. When they were done and the suds and water swirled to the drain Tog took a towel and wiped his hands. "This project Brad mentioned, I think there's more to it than you're telling." Jonathan said nothing; it didn't take long to understand that when Tog spoke he did not always expect a response or an answer. Tonight, get a good night's sleep. Tomorrow we head down to Greta's for breakfast and to pick up materials. You okay with working on the weekend?"

"Fine, weekend or week beginning, it's all the same to me. I'll hardly know the difference."

"Coffee's ready at 5:30. I'm going in to sit with the cat. You're welcome to join us."

"I'd like to get to know the cat, but I think I'll call it a day. Maybe make some notes; it's been a long day. Thank you Tog, for everything. You don't know anything about me, but you've taken me into your home. I appreciate it."

"So far I know what I know and it's good. Unless I see something bad, I'm going with the good. Rest well. Tomorrow you work for that meal." Tog smiled and headed down the hall.

◊

Jonathan continued his notes for a while. He made columns and tried to match what he knew with what he didn't know and concluded that although he didn't know what his life involved before, he was still himself and here and now was who he was. There must be someone or several or many he should miss, but he didn't know who. He wondered, but

55

assumed some must be missing him. They must be looking for him. He should be sad, but sadness has a base, a foundation and all he knows is himself and for now that's what it seems to be about. He tries again to bring a face to the name Lara, but still it is only a fading image. In that, there is sadness, but it has no breadth or body to it, only a longing.

He woke before five and heard Tog come down and soon he began to smell the coffee. Jonathan got up and in the bathroom, shaved with the kit Brad had gotten for him and then put on his shorts and tee shirt. He waited until 5:30 and then in stocking feet with his boots in hand and his fleece on but not zipped, he walked out to the kitchen. Bigcat, a large ball of fur settled in front of a dish of milk and Tog poured a cup of coffee. A second cup sat waiting on the counter. "Morning, sleep well? Help yourself." Tog had on tan pants and a blue shirt with accented stitching and button down pockets, and a brown leather belt with an intricate design cut into the leather. He had tied his hair back in a ponytail with several beaded strings. He turned and smiled at Jonathan and gestured to follow and headed toward the front rooms. Tog turned into the map room instead of the library and pulled the cord on a shade that hung halfway down and let it rise to the top.

"These maps, mostly Maine and Massachusetts, date back through the early settlement and pre-revolution years. I like the old ones that show Indian land, but collect all." He flared several open like a fan and sorted through until he came across

56

a specific one. "This one shows this land and the boundaries inhabited by the Maliseet." Tog sipped his coffee and looked over at Jonathan. "There's a lot of history between Maine and the Indian. Down in Bar Harbor there's a pretty decent museum, The Abbe Museum, been there?"

Jonathan looked up from the map. "Can't say that I have." Jonathan wasn't sure whether he had or not, but heard a distant familiarity in the name Bar Harbor.

"They do a good job. Some of it is hard to swallow, but it's history. The sum of our parts, bits and pieces gathered together, make us whole. Tog looked at Jonathan, his eyes, dark pools of brown, then turned and walked across the hall into the library. Bigcat came down the hall and curled up on the rug to begin what must be his daily routine. Jonathan sat on the window seat and looked out toward the road and the barn project. A low lying mist that had left the grass sparkling like a field of gems, burned off in the morning sun. Beads of condensation, warmed and set free by the gathering warmth, rolled off the Ranger and the hood of the pick-up.

"Quiet morning, is it always this quiet?"

Tog leaned forward and scratched Bigcat's neck. "Quiet is good. Out here if things aren't quiet, well, something's probably amiss, or someone's headed in. You up for Greta's breakfast? Then we'll head over and pick up framing. More can come out when the fence posts arrive. They'll be delivered."

"Sounds good to me," Jonathan stood and gestured with his cup, "Mind?"

"Help yourself. I'll wait for Greta's." Tog settled back in his chair and crossed his legs on the ottoman. "You best grab those coveralls. It's warming up but a bit snappy out there now—be warmer by 9 or so when the sun gets a little higher."

Jonathan returned to the kitchen and poured himself more coffee. He went to the bedroom and came out with the coveralls and hat in hand.

The front parking at Greta's overflowed so Tog pulled around back and parked the pick-up alongside a dumpster. He and Jonathan went in through a side door that came in beside the restrooms. It seemed everyone knew Tog and all happy they did. Hellos, miscellaneous comments and back slaps filled the air as they passed along behind those seated at the counter. The young woman that had waited on Jonathan and Brad, cleaning the same booth that Brad and Jonathan had sat at the day before, smiled as Tog slipped in to claim the booth. Not until she had finished wiping the table and setting down fresh mugs and silverware did she look up and see Jonathan.

"Hey, Tog, where've you been?" she asked and then turned toward Jonathan. The young woman paused for a minute, "Weren't you here yesterday with Brad?"

"Sure was." Jonathan smiled and turned his mug right side up.

"I'll be right back with coffee, new pot is brewing. Hey, Tog, I found an interesting map on E-bay. I bid on it and got it for $42.00. I'll show you sometime." She turned and headed behind the counter scooping up several checks with cash on her way.

"Greta's granddaughter, Becky, she looks damn young, but she graduated from college last year. She wants to stay in Maine so she's working here while she figures out what she wants to do."

"You get her into the maps?"

"Not really. She did a double major, Archeology and History. We discovered we had a common interest. She comes out to the house once in a while and rolls around the tables in that chair and studies the maps."

Becky came back and poured two cups of coffee. "So, what can I get for you?"

"Two eggs, loose and runny on toast, home fries, bacon, and tomato juice for me." Tog smiled at Becky and she turned toward Jonathan.

"Two eggs, over easy with pumpernickel toast…"

"…and sausage instead of bacon and cranberry juice." Becky finished for Jonathan and smiled. She turned and headed to another table before Jonathan could comment.

Several people stopped at the booth on their way out. Each time Tog introduced Jonathan: "This is my friend Jonathan. He's helping me with some fence work and a barn." They'd discuss different things and then move on with a handshake, a slap on Tog's shoulder or a squeeze of Tog's neck.

After breakfast Tog stepped into the kitchen and spoke with Greta and they shared a big hug. Outside the parking lot had thinned a bit, but others rolled in. The ride to the lumber yard took little time and Tog knew everyone there as well. Jonathan began to wonder how the man got anything done with all the time he had to take for hellos and small talk. Tog had two lists, one for today and one to come with the fence materials. They loaded the pick-up with 2x4's, 2x6's, some rough cut pine 5/4 and miscellaneous nails, screws and metal ties. With the load tied and secure they headed back toward Tog's. Before reaching the exit, Tog turned off the highway and swung through a side street coming into a shopping area. An assortment of stores from a Rite-Aid to a Donut shop to a couple general stores including a surplus store lined a small parking lot. Tog pulled in to a spot and turned the engine off. He reached into his pocket and took out a thick fold of bills and peeled five twenties from it. He handed the bills to Jonathan.

"I'll wait here. Go get yourself some supplies, pants, shirt, underwear, whatever you need. You'll earn that before dinner time tomorrow."

Jonathan took the money and looked at Tog.

"Go, we've got work to do."

# CHAPTER FIVE
*Shadow man*

Jonathan stepped over the cement stop and crossed a narrow strip of grass that had small trees held straight with guy wires then glanced up and down the store fronts choosing one to the left. As he walked he wondered why these two men Brad and Tog were so unconditionally kind. When he finds himself, will the man he finds be as kind? He smiled; how well they fit into the fictitious article he was supposedly writing.

Jonathan had chosen a surplus store and as he entered a bell hanging from the door trim rang when the door hit it. Inside a young man worked to the left sorting through a rack of military jackets, each a splotch work of browns and beiges; to the right a short portly man stood behind a counter leaning over a ledger of sorts following his finger as it moved down each column. Little half glasses rested forward on his nose and a green plastic visor you might expect a bookie at the horse tracks to wear encircled his forehead. He looked up, nodded and returned to his ledger.

Jonathan headed down an aisle passing racks of blue jean type pants and shelves made from stacked boxes that had folded chino pants. He walked sideways as if through a crowd and made his way through the abundantly stocked aisles. With the essentials of what he thought he needed, Jonathan did the math in his head rounding off the numbers and headed toward the counter.

The little man at the counter slid his ledger to the side and added Jonathan's items on an adding machine. With tax it totaled over a hundred dollars so Jonathan put one shirt to the side and the little man looked up and then tapped on his adding machine.

"That'll be $87.03" Jonathan handed him Tog's five twenty dollar bills.

"I've got the three cents," he said and reached into his pocket.

Outside, Jonathan looked for a drugstore and spotted a small Rite-Aid at the end of the stores. Inside he picked up a real tooth brush to replace the mini version in the survivor pack that Brad had bought for him, tooth paste and deodorant and then headed back to the truck.

Stepping onto the grassed median Jonathan watched as a gentleman about his age walked past with a boy who may have been eight or nine. The man looked down at the boy who clutched a large bag tight is his grip. The boy laughed when the man tousled his blond hair and then took the man's hand into his. Jonathan assumed it must be a boy with his grandfather. And he wondered if he had grandchildren—or children. He watched as the man and boy disappeared into the lines of parked cars and curling the fingers on his left hand he thought of Lara, certain she remained the answer to many if not all of his questions. He took a deep breath as if to prepare himself and continued across the grass toward Tog's truck.

Tog sat making notes in a small book with a pencil so whittled down it hardly fit between his massive fingers. He looked up when Jonathan opened the door and closed his book then set it in the cove where the dashboard curved in to house the speedometer and other gauges. "All set?" Tog looked at Jonathan as he turned the key in the ignition

"Good to go!" Jonathan tucked his bag under his legs on the floor then reached around and pulled the seat belt across his chest and buckled it.

Back at Tog's three llamas had come down from the back height of the land and were grazing around the barn site and looked up when they drove in. When Tog pulled forward and began to back toward the barn foundation they meandered away with little concern. Tog backed over the rutted ground and the load slapped in the back of the pickup. Cooler now than it had been at Greta's, Jonathan appreciated the coveralls. He pawed through his bag and found the new gloves he had bought. Tog grabbed a pair of yellowed, oil stained leather gloves from the dash and got out. He untied the rope from his side and tossed the rope across the load and Jonathan unhooked it from tie downs on his side and tossed it back. Four saw horses sat to one side and they began to stack the framing across them. Tog released two bungee cords that held a tarp over a pile. Under the tarp a large tool box, a generator and a shallow long box with power tools leaned one against the other. He pulled the generator from the pile and removed the gas cap. Jonathan picked up a gas can next to the tool box and handed it to Tog then untangled a long heavy duty electrical cord in the box and stretched it toward the foundation. Everything needed seemed to be there albeit in a bit of disorder and somewhat tangled. A lot like himself, Jonathan thought—a bit tangled and in a state of disorder, but all there otherwise. He looked at the boards lying against the foundation bolts and headed back to the power tools to find a drill. Tog adjusted something on the generator then stood, placed a foot on the frame and pulled the starter rope. It sputtered and stopped. He adjusted something else and pulled again. This time it ran for a second, back fired and stopped.

"Too bad they don't make those things electric so you could just plug 'em in." Tog stood up, smiled and shook his index finger in the air as though scolding a child. A few more adjustments and the generator started and gradually worked itself into a smooth pace, probably condensation in the gas tank.

Jonathan found a square and had started to mark the plates

to be drilled when Tog came over.

"You've done this before!" From the far corner of the barn's intended floor he retrieved a heavy plastic bag and dumped washers and nuts onto a plastic bucket cover then went to the tools and came back with a socket set. By lunch time, which extended past twelve almost to one, they had the plate on and one wall framed and ready to stand. They had accomplished a lot, but not such that Jonathan felt he had earned his clothes.

Lunch followed the same routine of foraging as the day before, tasty and filling just the same. Bigcat wound in and out of their ankles as they ate and Tog poured him more milk and refreshed a small bowl of dry food. A UPS truck pulled into the driveway as they were headed back out and Tog and the driver exchanged a few words and a laugh and Tog took a brown envelope and set it on the rocker on the porch.

The afternoon went well. It surprised Jonathan when he picked up the framing gun and actually knew how to use it. When the day ended, sometime after five, all four walls were up and the top plate had tied them together. They had braced the walls and Tog had laid out a rafter template. When he rolled the generator back to the pile and dragged the brown tarp up over the tools, Tog looked up with a smile.

"Good day, you're paid up." Off to the northeast a few llamas hung out near a stand of aspens, but no sheep could be seen. At the porch, Tog retrieved the UPS envelope and headed in. He turned into the library and sat to take off his boots and

Jonathan did the same. He slipped on a pair of lined moccasins and Jonathan stood in his stocking feet. Tog opened a large woven basket and sorted through until he found a pair of sock slippers, wool blend with leather soles and tossed them to Jonathan.

"They should fit, they stretch." Tog headed into the kitchen and turned as he left. "You up for a glass of wine, got the hard stuff too, but never touch it. Indian thing you know," He laughed as he turned into the kitchen.

Certain that the big stuffed chair belonged to Tog, Jonathan settled into the wing back and reached to pull the ottoman over when Bigcat got up and half rolled , half walked  then settled himself across Jonathan's feet and ankles. Tog came in with two glasses of wine and a bowl of chips.

"Looks like you pass muster. Bigcat must want you to stay." Tog set the wine glasses on a small table. "Nights are still a bit cool up here, a fire should feel good." He glanced over at Jonathan and sat down and Jonathan got up and moved the big screen from in front of the fireplace. A wood box to the right had all he needed and he surprised himself with how proficient he was at starting a fire. He took his wine when he went back to his chair and gently slid his toes back under Bigcat who had only slightly moved when he got up.

Tog settled into his chair, his long legs stretched toward the fire and his ankles crossed one over the other. He held his wine glass, rocking it gently. "What's your family think of your writing project?"  Jonathan, caught off guard, hesitated wondering if he should just tell this man who had so willingly and openly befriended him his whole story. As much as it felt like it would be a relief to confide in someone, Jonathan for reasons he had not totally sorted out, held back.

"Family, well they aren't part of my immediate picture." Jonathan sipped his wine and looked toward the fire that had taken off and curled around and through the two pieces of split wood he had positioned above the kindling. He felt guilty being evasive with this man who had been nothing but kind to him. Tog said nothing more.

"How about you?" Jonathan turned back to face Tog. "Do you have family?"

"Mother is in assisted living; Dad was a B-52 tail gunner in Vietnam and died on my sixth birthday. Mom became a single parent—damn good one too. Had a twin brother Wynono, means first born, but lost him in high school." Tog delivered this in a matter-of-fact way. "Just me and Bigcat." Tog sipped his wine and watched the flames of the fire lap the edges of a log like a delicate tongue. Neither man spoke for several minutes then Tog adjusted in his chair and looked back at Jonathan, "It was a heart thing, no one knew it. He had an enlarged heart and died playing in a homecoming basketball game in our senior year. Had mine checked—it's good." Tog got up and took a long poker and reached over the fireplace screen to adjust the logs and added a third. He turned toward Jonathan and stooped to pat the cat. "You're a shadow man my friend." He stood up and went back to his chair.

"I'm a what?"

"A shadow man; I'm not seeing the real you just a shadow." Tog looked at Jonathan and their eyes met; for a moment the two men sat this way and said nothing. Mother hit a wall early in life," Tog said. "Maybe from working so hard. I took care of her as long as I could here in the old family home. She needed more than I could give her and now she's in a nice facility in Lincoln. Speaking of Mother, that UPS is from the home. Tog got up and went back to the map room where he had left the envelope. He opened it as he came back to his chair. He pulled out several papers and leafed through them quickly and then slid them back into the envelope. "They document everything—copies of a new med program." Tog tossed the envelope toward the window seat and it landed against a pillow.

"You married Jonathan?"

Jonathan glanced at the ring finger of his left hand and remembered the name Lara.

"I am. Lara, wife's name is Lara." Bigcat half raised himself and adjusted moving in what appeared a complete circle and laid back down exactly where he had been.

"Lara, she's fine about your little adventure?"

"I suspect in the end she will find it quite interesting, maybe a bit disturbing, but interesting just the same." Jonathan did not know for sure that he had a wife named Lara, but the reoccurring images and name suggested he did. With no reason not to trust Tog, Jonathan ached to share his fears and apprehension with someone. He looked up at Tog and was about to speak when Tog rose up from his chair.

"You up for spaghetti and meatballs, made the sauce myself?" Tog got up and passed by Jonathan. "More wine?"

"With the spaghetti sounds great. What can I do?"

"Watch the fire."

Jonathan did watch the fire and as flames darted and tickled the stacked cord wood a small piece broke loose, floated and then was sucked up the chimney and inside Jonathan felt a renewed emptiness and longing that although intense and real remained undefinable.

# CHAPTER SIX
*Pieces of a Puzzle*

A nne Vaillancourt laid the evidence bags on her desk. She separated the bag with the scrap of yellow cloth and the one with the cell phone clip from the others. Turning to her computer she brought up a contact list and found numbers for UPS and Fed Ex. She punched in the number for Fed Ex and after a few transfers she connected with a dispatch supervisor. Identifying herself, she asked that the driver whose route included Highway 2A call her. She repeated this with UPS. She labeled a large manila envelope "Andersen / Patrick and Lara." dated it then scooped her bags into it and placed it in her top drawer. The bits and pieces she had revealed very little and even the best of detective work wasn't going to tell her too much. She needed more and hopefully someone saw something that might account for the torn cloth and disturbed shoulder on that stretch of highway.

Anne rolled backward in her chair and looked at the picture of her husband and daughter, which sat on a side table against the wall. On the wall above this, hung the picture that had run in the paper, with her father pinning on her badge. How helpless Lara Andersen must feel, she thought, just waiting and unable to do anything more. The springs on her desk chair squeaked as she rocked back and forth. Certain Lara must be settled in town by now Anne picked up the phone and dialed Lara's number. Anne had nothing more to tell her, but felt a call might be comforting for Lara as she waited for her daughter. Lara answered on the first ring. She explained that her daughter was on her way and that they would stay in Lincoln and wait to hear from Anne. Lara sounded calm and in control, but Anne heard the strain and an edge in her voice. Anne promised to call by eleven the next morning or earlier if anything turned up. At half past four Anne hung up. With little more that she could do, Anne finished shuffling papers and folders on her desk and prepared to leave when the phone rang. She picked up the handset from the black phone on her deputy's desk and pushed the button for "Chief."

"Could I speak to Chief Vaillancourt, please?"

"This is Chief Vaillancourt." Anne stepped around the deputy's desk and swung the chair around and sat down.

"Chief, this is Rodney Quinn. I drive for UPS. My supervisor told me to call you about my route this morning.

"Thank you for calling, Mr. Quinn. I'm interested in knowing if you were on the Pine Creek section of 2A this morning between 7 and 10?"

Rodney Quinn paused and Anne could hear pages flipping. "Yes, I came through about 7:45, heading north."

"Did you see any vehicles on the side of the road, especially near the Turtle Pond area?" Anne jotted down Rodney's name, the time of his call and waited.

"I did, a brown, sort of a chocolate brown van with some kind of decal along the sides like flames or something. The windows were tinted. Late Ford I think. I figured someone had pulled over to sleep for the night. It's a long lonesome road."

Anne paused—she knew this van. "Mr. Quinn, did you notice anything else about this van?" The driver had nothing more to add. Anne wrote the name Derek Wilson and made repeated circles around it. "Thank you very much for getting back to me so quickly. You have been very helpful. Do you mind giving me a contact number in case I have more questions?"

Derek Wilson, no stranger to Anne's office or to many others for miles each way, had a reputation that ran far ahead of him, as did his father Pete's. Derek's Aunt Tammy graduated with Anne and remained one of those high school friends you held onto for life. She, like most, left Pine Creek, married and had her family in suburbia, returning every other year for the holidays. Pete never left and never developed much more ambition than he had in high school. He married, had a son, divorced, married, divorced and settled in with his beer and cheap whiskey to a life that shifted from unemployment to part time job and back. He frequently got into trouble, usually alcohol-related—a scuffle here and there. In an error of justice, he somehow ended up with custody of Derek, which was never good for either of them. Old secrets surfaced, much the same as they did graduation night at Turtle Pond, and Derek rebelled and took off. Eventually he would be dragged back, but little time passed before he left again. Now at eighteen and no real plan for the future, he usually slept in his van albeit more often than not parked on his father's adjacent woodlot. A bit of a con man, but fun and interesting, he drew innocent people into his wayward ways.

With all this on her mind, Anne drove the short distance to where Pete Wilson lived in his run down double-wide. She slowed as she rounded the curve, not surprised to see Derek's van backed into the sod drive of the wood lot. She stopped and debated whether or not to call for back up, but decided against it. She pulled up in front of Pete's door with her truck facing toward the chocolate van. When she stepped onto Pete's broken down front porch she could see him slouched in an overstuffed chair in front of the TV. He turned when she knocked and leaned forward to set a beer on a table littered with several days' worth of chip bags and TV dinner trays.

"Well, I'll be damned." Pete stood, staggered and got his bearings. "Social call, Chief, or has Fuck-Up done something again?"

"Pete, I need to talk to Derek, is he here?" Anne stood outside the screened door and watched as Pete wobbled closer.

Pete looked out the door toward the woodlot. "Van is, I suspect Fuck-Up is too." Pete pulled a crushed pack of camels out of his soiled blue jeans and struggled to light one with a Bic lighter. He half turned and exhaled smoke, but most of it went through the screened door and into Anne's face. She turned from this as well as the smell of Pete that had taken over what space remained between them. Clearly it had been sometime since he'd seen the inside of a shower or attended to any other personal hygiene.

"Thank you." Anne turned from the door, stopping when Pete started to come out. She held up her hand. "I'd like you to stay here, Pete." The sternness of her voice and her look was enough, even in his inebriated state, for Pete to know she meant business.

None of Derek's mischief ever involved a weapon of any kind, but Anne instinctively unbuckled the flap that secured her service revolver. She stepped to the center of the road so she could approach the van from the front and move around to the sliding side door.

Anne heard sounds from inside, muffled sounds that she couldn't identify. She banged on the tinted window and announced herself. "Police, open the door, Derek." Anne heard a bang as something or someone fell and then the van rocked. Fearing Derek had headed for the driver's seat, Anne yanked down on the handle and the unlocked door slid open.

On the floor, fallen backward between a box and some kind of camp table, William Dunbar regained his balance. Anne recognized William as one of the high school's freshman. His had his shirt off and his pants were unzipped. Anne shook her head and turned to where Derek tried to climb into the driver's seat. With his legs tangled in his pant legs, he struggled to pull them above his knees and the tails of his torn yellow shirt had caught in the seat belt anchor.

"Don't, Derek. Stop right there." Anne quickly stepped one foot into the van. Derek crumbled into the passenger seat and smacked his fist against the dashboard. Anne told William Dunbar to sit on the ground next to the van and ordered Derek to come out. Whatever Anne interrupted going on between Derek and William seemed to be consensual although William was under age. Regardless, given Derek's attempt to escape out the front of the van, Anne though it wise to fit him with handcuffs until she gained full control. As she did this, Pete came staggering from the trailer.

"What the fuck is…"

Anne pointed her finger directly into Pete's face. "Back, Pete, get back." Pete backed up and stumbled on a pile of cut wood. With the scene secured and everyone under her control, Anne walked the two boys to her truck and had them sit on the ground at the front tire. William sat crying and wiping his face with his tee shirt. Anne reached in for her hand set and called into her deputy who was on duty at the station until 9 P.M.

"…and get a tow truck out here. I want this van impounded. I'll wait for you and you can transport these two."

"William Dunbar, this isn't going to go over well."

"Tell me about it. The reverend is not going to be happy." Anne signed off and looked down at the two boys. Derek slid his feet in the dirt, making parallel troughs and muttering to himself, William continued to whimper. "Zip up your pants, William," Anne said, "and put your shirt on."

◊

A road service truck towed the van to the lot next to the police station. In the morning the steps to obtain a search warrant would be completed. The first two things Anne found in the van were a rumpled hat and a unique walking stick with medallions from a number of national and state parks affixed to it attesting to the owner's wanderings. Anne assumed these to be those mentioned by Lara Andersen. In a cigar box, wrapped in elastic bands taken from supermarket produce Anne found a wallet and a cell phone. The contents of the wallet, loose in the box, included two credit cards, an Anthem medical card, a driver's license issued to Patrick Andersen, $32.00 in cash, two business cards, and a gold wedding band. On the console a padded plastic envelope like one used to mail a CD contained a rumpled handkerchief and a prescription bottle of Midazolam. Anne also collected grass, dirt and sod clumps from the floor mats for additional analysis. The search warrant would be required to look further, but she had evidence that linked the van to what she found on the trail. In addition, Derek's torn shirt matched the scrap of cloth she had found and the van matched the description provided by the

UPS driver. Anne had enough to hold them for further questioning.

Both boys were read their rights and Deputy Flannigan transported Derek to the holding cell. Anne released William into the custody of his parents, Reverend and Mrs. Arthur Dunbar. William, through a continuous flow of tears, waived his right to an attorney and provided a bountiful flow of information and detail. Derek said nothing. Aside from the fact that Derek was a legal adult and William was a minor, Anne would have been happy not to discuss how the boys were found, but it would come up sooner or later.

Although a bit convoluted and complicated, in essence, as William described the events, what had happened out on the trail near Turtle Pond was a bungled robbery attempt where the boys intended to sedate Patrick Andersen, rob him, and take him to an ATM machine. With little knowledge of the drug they were using, they used too much. Patrick's knees buckled and he crumbled to the ground. Unable to get him to stand, they panicked and dragged him to the van and drove to an isolated location and left him. William had gone back to set Patrick's glasses next to him. They drove around most of the day smoking pot. William insisted that he begged Derek to go back and check on Patrick. Derek refused to go back and eventually they landed back at Derek's father's lot. Derek insisted that Patrick would be fine. Soon the gentle swirl of apathy brought on by the pot calmed William and they were content until Anne interrupted the culmination of their mutual highs.

◊

Late the next morning, with William in the back seat of Anne's big Ford's extended cab, sandwiched between his parents; they drove to the spot where William said they had left Patrick Andersen, almost ten miles north of the small trail where Patrick had walked to his picnic rock. William directed the chief to a logging road and explained how Derek had cut the cable so they could drive through. Anne got out of her vehicle and unhooked the coat hanger that held the broken cable. She drove the truck down the logging road to the end where a chewed up spot on the left provided a turnaround of sorts. With William in the lead and his parents to his side, they walked to a point where the pines were tall and the sun shone through in myriad shades of green. William pointed out where he had folded and set Patrick's glasses. There were insignificant signs that someone had been there, but nothing more. Walking back, the chief instructed the Dunbars to walk in the very center as she scanned each side for anything out of the ordinary.

When Anne pulled the truck up onto the shoulder and waited while William fixed the make-shift cable she noticed a sign hung from hooks across the street at the entrance of an unblocked drive. Nothing about the drive was unusual, but when Anne pulled onto the pavement she decided to drive down it. She rounded a gentle curve passing by a low area and came upon a cabin tucked into the trees, remarkably similar to Lara Andersen's cottage.

"Wait here," she said to the Dunbars. She walked around the outside of the cabin, down one side, along the back and then up the other side to the front. Everything seemed secure, not yet opened for the season. Stepping onto the porch, she rocked the first rocking chair and its chain tether dragged in the dust. Looking at a second chair, the chief noticed a similar mark in the accumulated dust and blown leaves. She knelt and looked more closely and then stood and turned toward the door and then to the folded shutters secured against the building with cross bars. Under the farthest window a small pile of white chips of some kind hung suspended in a cobweb that stretched from the front siding to a deck board. She reached down and took a small piece of the material in her fingers and pinched it, rubbing it into a powder paste. She smelt this and then brushed it off. The dry moldy smell reminded her of an old towel. Anne stood up and then lifted the cross bar that secured the shutters out of its yokes. When she pulled the shutters open, she saw where the glazing of one pane had been removed, but the glass remained in place and secured with small metal points. She shaded her eyes with her hand and peered in through the window at a cottage, clean and neatly put to bed. She began to turn away and then looked back. One chair sat askew, very much out of character with everything else in its proper place. On the table a piece of paper was weighted with a small white plate, no doubt a reminder list for spring opening probably even including the re-glazing of a window. Anne returned to her truck, with the cob web and the chain markings still on her mind. She settled into her seat, glanced back at the Dunbars and then pulled her seat belt across and buckled it. Anne sat for a moment and then took the mike from its yoke on the dash.

A full minute passed before Deputy Flanagan answered the radio. "Flanagan here, go ahead." The voice crackled over the radio.

"Dick, see if you can find contact information for someone named Haskell who has a cabin about ten miles north of Turtle Pond on 2A. If you can, get ahold of them and tell them I need to enter their cabin as part of an investigation."

"Are you there now?"

"I am."

"Chief, that's Brett Haskell's place. He and his brother share it. They use to hunt from it, but now it's a family getaway. I'll give him a call."

"Good. I'm going to run the Dunbars back to their place and then call Lara Andersen." Anne turned toward the Dunbars. I'll take you back to your house, but I'll need William again. We're waiting for an analysis of that drug. You still don't want to tell me where it came from, William?"

William hung his head and then raised it slowly. "Derek had it. I don't know where he got it." William slumped down and crossed his arms across his chest but sat up when his father elbowed him in the side.

Anne backed the big Ford around and then pulled forward

past a canoe on sawhorses and headed out the road. As she passed the marsh area, Deputy Flanagan came over the radio.

"Chief, I caught Bret Haskell in his shop. He says there's a key in a box attached under the canoe's stern seat. He said go ahead in if you need to. I told him you'd call later and tell him what was up."

"Great. I'm pulling out, but I'll take a look." The dirt drive road was too narrow to turn on so Anne continued to the road and turned and then headed back in. Anne found the box under the stern seat, a regular hide-a-key box with a sliding top. A piece of metal had been glued to the seat so the box's magnet could stick to it. Anne instructed the Dunbars to stay in the truck. At the door, she twisted the wooden lock and pulled the screen door open. She lifted the rubber flap and fitted the key into the padlock and turned. The lock snapped open and she eased the door open. As it had appeared through the window, the cabin was neat and clean with everything in its proper order. Anne walked around the cabin and each room and every corner had been left neat and clean to a fault. She could smell coffee and she looked around for a can of coffee or a coffee pot. Under the sink she found an old camp percolator. Although empty, condensation covered the little glass top. When she removed the top there was a strong, fresh smell of coffee. At the table she straightened the chair and picked up the paper held by the small plate. It wasn't a "to do" list and Anne began to read it. The note explained why someone had entered the cabin and offered an apology of sorts signed. The note included a list of items taken and had been signed, Jonathan.

Well, Jonathan could be Patrick Andersen. He seems to be well and is eating and now I know what he is probably wearing, but although I know this much he doesn't seem to know much about himself. Thinking it through, Anne felt certain Jonathan and Patrick Andersen were one and the same.

# CHAPTER SEVEN
### Connecting the Dots

Anne did not recognize the voice that answered when she called Lara Andersen, but assumed it must be Lara's daughter.

"Yes ma'am, this is her daughter Lucy. Let me get my mom." Anne could hear a door open and Lucy call to her mother. In a minute Lara picked up the phone sounding a little out of breath.

"Did you find Patrick?" Anne heard the anxious tone in Lara's voice.

"No, we haven't actually found him, but I have good reason to believe he's okay. We do know what happened, when, and where." Anne paused allowing Lara time to absorb this. "I feel very confident that he is well, but I don't know where."

"What happened is he hurt, what happened?" Lara's voice was shaking now and Anne could hear Lara's daughter's muffled voice comforting her.

"Lara, I should come down so we can talk. I'll explain everything. Anne waved at Deputy Flanagan as he stood at the office door with a large manila envelope in his hand.

"Chief, this is Lucy. Mom had to sit down."

"Is she okay?"

"I think so. She couldn't sleep last night. She's pretty wound up."

"Lucy, I'm headed down to see both of you. Tell your Mom, so far the news is good. We're going to find your Dad."

"Thanks, Chief. We're in room 18."

"Good, I'll see you in about an hour.

Anne hung up the phone. Deputy Flanagan stood waiting in front of her desk.

"Medical report." He set the envelope on her desk and raised his eyebrows.

Anne unwound the red string that secured the flap of the envelope. She slid out a small stack of papers with a formal letter clipped to the top. She read the letter and then flipped through a few of the pages looking at selections highlighted in yellow.

"Have you ever heard of Midazolam, Dick?"

"Can't say I have, but it doesn't sound like your run of the mill street drug."

"The report says it's used for conscious sedation and maintenance of anesthesia. It is known to cause anterograde amnesia, but not necessarily retrograde amnesia–basically memory during a procedure but not necessarily before. There's a note that says: see case report KNL-51." Anne flipped to the first page with highlighted material and found case report KNL-51. She read down tracing the lines with the eraser end of her pencil. "It says a 61-year old man had been given Midazolam and he showed evidence of memory loss and was unable to state his or his wife's name." Anne continued down the page flipping it over and going to the next. "They gave him an injection of Flumazenil, whatever that is and both his short term and long term memory returned."

"This is what you found in the van and you think they used it on Patrick Andersen?"

"That's what it looks like." The chief gathered the papers and slid them back into the envelope. "Where in hell do you think those two got hold of a drug like this?" The chief rolled her chair back and stood up. "I'm headed to meet with Lara Andersen and her daughter. See if you can find any reports of a pharmacy break-in, a doctor's office, anyplace that may have reported this stuff stolen. I'm going to have another talk with Derek. We'll need to get those charges filed before this evening. I'm not sure when he'll be sent to county, but I expect soon."

Derek's cell wasn't much of a cell at all, but more an oversized lockable closet. Balanced on a straight chair with his feet against the wall, he rocked the chair back and forth on its rear legs. The steel grid door, made by a local welder, locked the make- shift cell more often than not used for short periods when someone needed to calm down or sober up.

"Pretty interesting drug you were playing with, Derek." Derek continued rocking the chair and didn't look up. "I'm not sure which will be heavier the charge for kidnapping and assault or the theft of this heavy duty drug. Guess that depends on how you came about having it." Derek looked over at the chief and let the chair settle onto all four legs, but said nothing. "Anything you want to tell me? We'll find out sooner or later but it'd be better for you if you helped out." Derek stood up and turned the chair so that the back faced the chief and sat back down. "Your choice, I guess the apple doesn't fall far from the tree." The chief turned to leave and Derek muttered something under his breath, but the Chief was pretty sure she didn't need or want to hear it.

On the way out the Chief retrieved her belt and service revolver from a hook in the front office and took her uniform jacket as well. Deputy Flanagan sat at his desk working at a computer.

"Probably won't be back until 4 or 5. If anything serious surfaces, give me a call."

The deputy swung around from the computer. "Will do."

In her truck, Anne set the envelope with the medical report and the note that Patrick left at the Haskell's cottage and a second with Patrick's belongings on the seat and then started the engine and pulled out. The cool afternoon reminded Anne that Patrick had taken a fleece from the cabin. She wondered which direction he headed. If he heads west he heads toward the rugged wilderness of the Maine Mountains. East eventually takes him to New Brunswick and to the coast and south takes him to the rest of the world—a more civilized world where there are malls and cities. Leaving the Haskell cabin, Patrick or Jonathan as he is calling himself would have been on the northbound side of the road and with no reason to cross probably headed north. North the towns are sparser and eventually there is Canada. But not knowing where you are all directions would be somewhat the same

If he doesn't know who he is or where he's from, what will he look for? Judging by what he took from the cabin, the note he left and his obvious care for the Haskell's property, the man seems organized and although he may not have a fully laid out plan Anne is pretty sure he is working one out.

She smiled thinking back to how her father would say: "Don't go off half-cocked." As a young girl she never knew what he meant, but eventually the concept of getting all the information together, assessing a situation and then getting your ducks all in a row became the essential recipe for success. Memories of her father's lessons more often than not shaped her own investigative procedures. Again she remembered his advice:

"The Seven P's:" *Proper Prior Planning Prevents Piss Poor Performance*

Patrick Andersen's adherence to fundamental proper planning enhanced Anne's caring for the man and exceeding generic police work. She could imagine talking with him and admiring his deductive reasoning and proactive approach to his predicament. She missed her father.

## CHAPTER EIGHT
### Bits and Pieces

A nne saw very few other vehicles on the highway most of the drive to Lincoln, the trailer trucks in both directions appeared more a part of the scenery than traffic. She arrived at the Travel Lodge at 1:05 and pulled up in front of room eighteen. Lara Andersen came through the door before Anne could get out of her truck. A young woman almost the same height as Lara with short blond hair, wearing a quarter zip fleece and tan pants stepped from the room and put her arm over Lara's shoulder.

Anne introduced herself to Lucy, tucked the two envelopes and folder under her arm and followed Lucy and Lara into the motel room. The room looked like most you can find along the highway, but a little newer and with a little more attention to detail. Two queen beds and a good size table with two chairs and another sitting chair to the other side surprisingly fit without making you feel packed in a can of sardines. Lucy gestured toward the table.

Anne set her folder and envelopes on the table and went to one of the chairs. Lara perched on the edge of the bed and Lucy stood. Anne started right in knowing that the tension had been building since her call. "I have every reason to believe that your husband, your father is well," she began. "We know what happened, and a little more, but we have not found him."

"What happened? How do you know he is okay?" Lara sat with her legs close and she clenched her hands tightly in her lap. Lucy sat next to her mother and laid one hand on her mother's. Anne could see the effect the stress and a sleepless night had on Lara. The in control woman that Anne left at the cabin had been consumed and rightfully so. Anne hoped that the good information would provide some relief from the unknown.

"Patrick had gone to the picnic rock as you suggested but while there he encountered two teenage boys who intended to rob him. We believe they planned to take him to an ATM machine and have him withdraw money. We arrested the two boys and we recovered Patrick's wallet, his hat, and his walking stick." Anne reached into one of the envelopes and took out Patrick's wallet, cash, cards, and the wedding band recovered from the van and handed them to Lara. "I'll need these back," she said, "You may keep the ring."

"What did they do to him?" Lara held these in her hands

like someone might hold a rescued bird.

"They had a drug, Lara, a drug that is used for what is called conscious sedation. It's when a procedure is going to be performed but you don't want the patient to remember the trauma of the event. They used it on a cloth to subdue Patrick." Anne paused "They had no idea what they were doing and must have used too much and Patrick became unstable and incoherent. We know this because one of the boys is telling all he knows, but the other won't say a word. They panicked and dragged Patrick to their van and drove him about ten miles north where they left him in the woods."

"Do you think he's still in the woods?" Lucy gently rubbed her mother's hand.

"Not exactly." Anne reached into the envelope and took out the note Patrick left in the Haskell cottage. "We found this in a cabin near where he had been left. I believe Patrick wrote it." Anne handed the note to Lara and the look on Lara's face confirmed that she recognized the handwriting. Lucy leaned over her mother' shoulder and read the note with her.

"The medical report says that this drug can cause amnesia. I think the note is good evidence that Patrick is okay, but doesn't know who he is or where he is. I believe he spent the night in the Haskell cabin, but left very early. I suspect he is being cautious not knowing who did this to him and fearing that they might come back for him."

At this point silence fell over the room and hung like a threatening storm cloud. Lara continued to read and reread the note and Lucy stood up and walked to the window. Anne Vaillancourt sat quiet letting it all settle in. After several minutes, Lucy turned from the window. "What now? What do we do next?' Lara looked up at Lucy and then toward the chief and with hands now visibly shaking she gave the note back to Anne.

"There is a chance that Patrick is remembering bits and pieces, but they are probably fragmented tumbling together like in a kaleidoscope. Anne continued, sharing all she had discovered from her reading of the case study and other information her deputy had gathered. "For now, even though he doesn't know who he is, he is still himself, his values, his priorities and the way he thinks are all him. That's what I have to focus on and build on."

Anne set the envelopes to one side and brought a yellow folder forward and opened it. When we look for a suspect we do everything we can to determine what his next move will be, how he thinks and in essence get one step ahead of him or at least in step with him. I know the word sounds negative in today's politically correct world of language, but what we do is profile him. I need to do this with Patrick. I need to know how he thinks what he thinks whether he prefers hash browns or home fries, vanilla or chocolate, how he takes his coffee etc. I need to get to know him as closely as possible. I need you to tell me anything and everything that might help to define who Patrick is. Then I'm going to find him."

Lara leaned forward resting her face in her hands and Lucy

stood up and placed her hands on her shoulders. Lara drew her fingers to each side wiping away tears that had begun to form. She turned slightly toward Lucy and then patted Lucy's hands and stood up. "Let's get started."

Lucy sat down on the edge of the bed and her mother joined her. She looked at her mother and then at Anne. "Most people would describe Dad as serious, but he can be funny and is always witty. He's smart and quick and loves word games, I don't mean scrabble or cross words, I mean language and bantering back and forth."

"Patrick," Lara added, "well to say he is very neat and orderly would be an understatement. He likes things under control. He doesn't have to control things, but if he encounters things out of control he'll quickly step in."

"He likes cranberry juice and sausage instead of bacon and Dad likes people, but he doesn't like to be with just anyone. He used to quote Rod McKuen saying that people joined clubs today for the same reason they used to carry them."

The process started and Anne took notes for over an hour. Each little bit was crucial. Something totally unexpected might be the clue to turn her left instead of right.

## CHAPTER NINE
### *Making a plan*

Anne Vaillancourt got a call from Lucy at home early Saturday morning. "Good morning Chief. I'm sorry to bother you at home."

"No bother. Up here, home or office, there's not a lot of daylight between the two. What's up?" Anne turned from the phone. "Excuse me Lucy." She leaned toward her daughter strapped in her high chair at the table. "Mommy has to talk on the phone for a minute. Finish your pancake and then we'll get washed up. Sorry Lucy."

"Oh that's fine. Saturday morning is probably busy there." Lucy paused and then began again. "My sister Lynn arrived last night and we brought her up to date on everything. I explained how you want to "profile" dad and create something people might notice and recognize. Lynn's older, and well, first borns see more, she had a lot of things that will be good to include. We thought we could all talk together. We'll come to Pine Creek."

"Sounds great, you can come to the office. What time is good? The sooner we get something out there the better. I don't know how your Dad is traveling and how fast. All evidence and logic suggests he headed north so we need to get something in place that can intercept him. Don't forget the pictures."

"Good, we'll get there by ten if that works. Mom will too."

"I'll see you then. Give my best to your mom." Anne hung up the phone and made a quick note and then sat down with her daughter.

Clint Vaillancourt came in the side door, back from a run to the post office. "Saw Flanagan at the post office. He wants you to check your email. He said he found something that may be interesting." Clint leaned over and kissed his daughter on the head. She reached up and tried to grab his face, but Clint jumped back. "Yucky, syrup hands. Didn't Mommy give you a fork? Want to get cleaned up and ride to the dump with Daddy?" The little girl immediately strained to climb from her chair.

"Whoa, little one, hands and mouth first." Anne came from the sink with a warm cloth and began the recovery process after a fun breakfast of pancakes. When her husband and daughter finished loading the trash and headed for the dump, Anne sat down at her computer to check the deputy's email.

*Chief,*

*Some interesting facts about that drug - Apparently there was a break-in at a surgical clinic down near Bangor a couple of months ago. They caught the teenagers several days later after they were bragging about their little escapade at a pool hall. They made a deal and got off with little more than slapped wrists in exchange for telling what happened to the drugs they stole.*

*Seems they sold some marijuana and the drugs to a guy in Pine Creek that they got hooked up with through some other low lifes. They only had a first name, Pete.*

Anne added this to Derek's sputtering about when he will get out and her advising that a little help from him might speed things up. Anne felt certain the Pete from Pine Creek was Pete Wilson. No doubt when she presents this to Derek he'll see things a little more clearly. He most likely stole the drug from his father, no respect lost there.

Anne pushed print and then closed her email. So, Pete is dirty, what a surprise. Derek steals from his father, another big surprise. Other than the kidnapping and assault charge, that may or may not be something to get around, Derek may be in pretty deep. Messing with marijuana is one thing, messing with a controlled drug like midazolam is another story all together. Seducing a minor, well the Reverend and his wife may want to let that one fade away.

If charges are not filed against Derek he will have to be

released. The weekend will buy a little time and Anne expects with the evidence already presented that the state prosecutor will act quickly and Derek can be transferred as early as Monday. Other than whatever testimony he may decide to give, Derek has no further value in what Anne has to do in order to locate Patrick Andersen. The Dunbar boy will probably continue to cooperate and no doubt become a witness for the state.

Anne straightened her desk and pushed the chair in. She would check in with Deputy Flanagan at the station later, otherwise it looked like Saturday would be different than was planned.

◊

When Anne stopped at the office to check in with Flanagan, she found an overnight envelope from the prosecutor's office on her desk. Anne opened the envelope and scanned through the several pages. Derek had been charged and would be picked up at 8:30 on Monday for transport to his arraignment. Given that neither Derek nor Pete could post bail, Derek would spend some time in waiting at Warren. Anne placed a call to Lara and Lucy hoping to catch them before they left Lincoln. Lucy answered on the second ring.

"Good morning," Anne straightened things on her desk as she talked. "I'm glad I caught you."

"Lynn's here and we're just waiting for Mom and headed for breakfast. What's up?" Lucy sounded tired. No doubt the talking went late into the night.

"Would eleven instead of ten be okay for you?"

"Sure, that's fine. Is something wrong?"

"Oh, no, just some loose ends I want to get out of the way. Come to the library across the street from my office, there's a nice little conference room we can use." Anne wanted Derek out of sight and out of contact. She didn't want his presence to further antagonize the situation.

"Fine, we'll see you at 11."

Anne went in and told Derek that charges had been filed and that he would be picked up and transported to his arraignment on Monday.

"Where's my lawyer?" Derek stood with his fingers wrapped in the grille of the cells door.

"We read you your rights. The court will appoint a lawyer." Derek slumped down and sat on the floor, a more quiet and subdued Derek than a day ago.

◊

Lara, Lucy and Lynn arrived right at eleven and Anne met them at the library door. Lucy, tall and thin, looked very much like her mother. Tall like her sister, Lynn had longer blond hair tucked behind her ears, a striking girl, with blue eyes that glittered when she spoke and smiled. A fit and trim woman, yet more full bodied than her sister. Anne had never seen Patrick, but assumed Lynn favored him.

After being introduced to Lynn, Anne led them to a small

conference room off the main corridor where there was a long table with chairs.

"Please, sit down.

Lara settled into a chair that Lynn had pulled out for her. Lucy had a folder and a worn envelope which she set on the table and Lynn took out a pad and a pen.

"First let me tell you that we don't really have any new information. We know where they got the drug, but that doesn't change anything.

"Lucy said you think he headed north. Why do you think that?" Lynn challenged as she jotted something down on her pad.

"Well he came out of the Haskell cabin on the northbound side of the road. With no reason to want either north or south it seems logical that he wouldn't have crossed the highway. It's not scientific, but seems to make sense. I won't ignore south, but I want to concentrate north."

Lara leaned forward and rested her arms on the table. "What do you intend to concentrate on?"

"I think Patrick is being cautious. He doesn't know what happened to him or who did it and he is probably worried they are looking for him. We want to find him, but not scare him. We need to draw him in where we can get close without him running. It's going to be delicate."

"Why," Lara blurted out, "should he run from us?"

"Because, I'm sorry Lara, but he doesn't know who you are." Anne looked at Lucy and then at Lynn.

Lynn doodled on her pad. "How do we do it?"

"Carefully, we'll make fliers with pictures of Patrick." Anne stood up and continued. "I want it to say "Have you seen this man?" and under the pictures we'll put his name. I don't want to mention amnesia or your names or even me."

"Why?" Lynn offered a challenge and Lucy remained quiet. "What about having the state police issue a "Silver Alert? Isn't that what they do when a senior citizen goes missing?" Lynn challenged.

"Sure if Patrick had wandered off, if he didn't know that something had been done to him, but I expect he knows he was some kind of victim and is afraid. The amnesia complicates things because if we mention the amnesia we set him up as a possible victim all over again. I think it is a given that the flier will suggest the police are looking for him , but otherwise making it a police issue may suggest he is dangerous in some way whoever might be helping him may fear him. Once we get at least some direction we can bring in more of a police presence."

"Where do these fliers go?"

"To truck stops, diners, restaurants, and police stations, but the "profile" for a lack of a better word will go only to police."

"And this is going to bring Dad home?" Lynn rocked her pen between two fingers and looked at Anne and then at her sister.

"Not exactly, what I hope it does is keep him from running and alerts us to where he is so we can, it's a start."

Lara sat back in her chair and straightened her back "When do we start?"

"I can get them printed this morning and have some faxed out this afternoon." Anne sat back and looked toward Lara.

Lara glanced over at Lynn with a look intended to stop any further challenge Lynn may have been planning. "Let's get started. Lynn, give her the pictures and let's make this profile."

They outlined a profile that included everything that distinguished Patrick form someone else; generally neat even in work clothes, clean shaven, polite, can be quiet but is witty, is a Democrat, is a veteran, has numerous skills in carpentry and general home renovations, likes animals, friendly, avoids confrontation, and the list went on. The girls and Lara made a cut and paste collage with several pictures of Patrick. He may or may not be wearing a hat because Anne found his in Derek's van so they included pictures with and without. Anne ran these on the office printer and after making some adjustments and deciding to scan them onto the computer instead of copying them she ended up with a clear and crisp flier. "Have You Seen This Man?" ran across the top and below the pictures it read "Patrick Andersen" and below that in parenthesis, recalling the note found in the Haskell camp, Anne added: "Sometimes calls himself Jonathan." Lynn argued that it should say something like "we miss you, please come home" but Anne reaffirmed her belief that they need to get close and then draw him in. Anne said the fliers would be delivered and information from the profile given to the business owners but not posted. Anne's number appeared on the bottom.

## CHAPTER TEN
### *Headed north*

When Anne Vaillancourt said good-by to the Andersen sisters and their mother, she promised to call as soon as anything new came up. She called several chiefs of police and explained the profile she was faxing and asked that Bangor deliver one to the manager at the big Dysart truck stop. Fearing that the State Police might launch a generic, canvassing approach that might scare Patrick in the way she was trying to avoid, she didn't involve them yet. She was walking a fine line, but jurisdictional authority would prevail. The time spent with Lara and Patrick's daughter had made Anne feel close and involved. Maybe it was memories of her own father or maybe intuition, but she decided not to hand this task over to her deputy. She decided to drive north toward Houlton and hand-deliver fliers to restaurants, gas stations and whatever else looked like a likely stop for a man heading north with nowhere to go. She put fliers into large manila envelopes and added a note typed on department stationary.

*We are looking for this man.*

*There is no warrant and he is not dangerous.*

*He may not be certain of his own identity and may be scared.*

*Please do not post, but advise and review with appropriate staff.*

*Call if you know of his whereabouts*

Anne signed the bottom of the flier and both her department phone and cell phone were listed. On the outside of the envelope she stamped the upper left corner with her department address and hand wrote: *For Management* in the center.

When Deputy Flanagan arrived, Anne briefed him on the plan and said she was headed north but would check in before six. At home they expected her by six and she would call if she expected to be late.

The beautiful spring day in northern Maine quickly warmed with the afternoon sun; Anne took her uniform jacket off, folded it and laid it on the seat. From a small tray on the dash she retrieved her sunglasses. There wasn't a lot to see on the first few miles heading north on Rte. 2; she passed by the old trail that led out to the rock where Patrick had been taken and then past Haskell's camp on the right. Farther up, she passed the road that headed out to Pete Wilson's. Whether

Pete would be charged for possession remained to be determined, but Derek's immediate future appeared certain. If the boy had had any guidance things might have turned out different.

As Anne drove, she thought about the Andersen sisters and how different they were. Lucy's warm and engaging demeanor stood in sharp contrast to Lynn's confrontational standoff presence. Maybe there was something to the argument that first borns are generally held more accountable while the second third or beyond benefitted from a softening of the parenting. Certainly her older brothers and older sister felt that. They called her "Daddy's girl" and argued that he was easiest on her. Anne smiled realizing that although she never bought into the fact that her dad dealt with her with a softer hand, she cherished the term Daddy's girl. Patrick Andersen's absence clearly left an open wound in his family and Anne felt drawn to them and eager to bring everyone back together.

Several miles north of Wilson's road a small gas station and mini-convenience store were tucked in some pines in front of a group of cabins long abandoned to the weather and nature. There wasn't much left of any of it, but it sat far enough from anything else that truckers and travelers generally stopped for coffee, snacks or just the bathrooms, which, surprisingly enough, were kept up quite well and happily made available to all. Anne pulled in and stopped at the pumps. You had a choice of full-service or self-service, whichever came first. Anne pumped her own gas and then went inside. Bev and Phil

Daggett owned what remained of Shady Pines and Anne saw Bev in back on a stool getting something from a shelf. Phil stood behind a counter where a small grill, a microwave and some kind of sandwich machine sat at the ready. Phil turned when Anne walked in.

"Hey Chief, what brings you up this far, out sightseeing?" Anne smiled. She and Phil had been in school together; he played varsity basketball as a freshman when she was a senior.

"Business, Phil. Trying to find a man that may have passed by here."

Anne took out the flier and laid it on the counter.

"What'd he do?" Phil leaned down, which was necessitated by the fact that he was over six foot five. He adjusted his glasses up on the bridge of his nose. Bev came from the back room and stood next to Phil and smiled up at Anne.

"Seen this fellow in here?' Phil asked turning toward Bev, and looking up at Anne, "Is he a bad one?"

"No, not at all we think he may be uncertain as to who he is and be travelling a little scared."

"You mean like amnesia?"

"Sort of." Anne paid for her gas and asked Bev and Phil to keep an eye out for Patrick and call if they saw or heard about him. She left the flier and asked that they post it and share it with regulars who stop in.

Anne drove several miles before she came to her next stop at an engine repair shop and a woodworkers shop. In each case, Anne explained the flier and left the same instructions.

After a while, the woods thinned a bit and a few more houses and signs of life appeared along the highway. On the right, a quintessential diner with the obligatory stainless steel railroad style car and attached wooden structures came into view. Anne had been here before on her way back from somewhere, but not in uniform. As the afternoon waned, the parking lot had filled and Anne knew it to be a favorite for truckers and locals alike. She pulled off to the side and parked next to a ten wheeler loaded with plywood. When Anne walked in she attracted a notable amount of attention. She wasn't sure if it was because the law walked in or because the law was female. At a booth near the front windows, Anne slid in adjusting her service revolver so it would slide along the vinyl seat.

An attractive young girl wearing blue jeans and a printed t-shirt came from behind the counter and stood in front of her.

"What can I get for you?" She had a pleasant smile and a spirited voice.

"Coffee, black. What's left for pastry?"

The young girl turned and looked back toward the window that separated the counter from the kitchen. "Well, what's left you don't really want, but there is some better than average pecan pie."

Anne smiled, "A piece of better than average pecan pie sounds perfect. " The girl started to turn. "...and I need to talk to the owner, is that Greta?"

"It is Greta, but she just left and won't be back until 4:30 tomorrow morning. I'm her granddaughter, assistant manager of sorts when she's not here, plain Becky when she is. Anything I can help you with?"

"Maybe, let me see that pie and we can talk."

Anne sat the envelope with the flier to the side and took out her cell phone and slid the little switch to silent. She doubted that she'd get home by six; she'll call from the truck when she left. Becky hardly looked old enough to be out of school never mind in charge of a diner. Anne watched as she headed around the end of the counter where everyone seemed to know her and most appeared to be regulars. Outside truckers started to pull in for an evening meal. There wasn't any order to the parking other than parallel, but all seemed to get inside the sign's posts and well off the road. The truckers of all sizes and shapes and both genders filtered and all seemed to know someone already seated. The ones that didn't head directly to the restroom gathered around the counter or a table as though they had arrived at old home week.

Becky returned with Anne's pie and coffee, set them in front of her and glanced back at the counter.

"Looks like you're going to get busy," Anne said.

"In a bit. They'll all talk for a while then settle down. It's the same thing each day, just a different group, like an endless high school reunion."

"Looks like you know everyone."

"Pretty much, the locals come in for breakfast, sometimes lunch and the truckers on and off all day long."

Anne cut into her pie and slid her coffee to the side. "Many strangers stop in?"

"Not this early in the season. A little later and we get the travelers. Now it's usually Greta's regulars." Becky turned when she heard her name mentioned up near the counter. "Guess I better get over there."

Anne nodded and smiled with a mouth full of what lived up to Becky's claim to be truly better than average pecan pie. When she finished, Anne found Becky up at the counter and waited for her at the cash register tucked in at the door end. Becky, pouring coffee and taking orders, appeared to be carrying on several conversations at once. She smiled at Anne and nodded. Several truckers glanced toward Anne and then went back to their meals and conversations.

"Sorry," Becky said when she spotted Anne at the register. "They're full of it when they finally stop, unwinding from the road I guess."

"No problem. Is it just you and your cook?"

"Yes and no. There's a little group that hangs around 'til closing. They say they haven't anything else to do, but truth be told I think Greta put them up to it."

"Well the pie was as good as you promised. I'd appreciate it if you could give this to Greta. There's a note inside explaining and my number as well." It wasn't a good time to explain the flier and Anne thought it best that Greta see it first.

"Will do" Becky took the envelope and laid it on a pile on a counter behind her that had an assortment of invoices and delivery slips. "It's her desk of sorts." Becky smiled at Anne.

Anne turned to leave and bumped into a UPS delivery man. "Whoa, sorry," the man said and stepped to the side.

"My fault." Anne smiled and headed out through the door held open by the delivery man with his free hand while balancing a box in his other.

"I hope those are the stove parts," Becky took the box from the driver and pretended to shake it.

Outside Anne stopped to wave to Becky, but Becky had turned and to set the box on Greta's "desk."

## CHAPTER ELEVEN
### Sunday in Lincoln

Tog's spaghetti and meatballs provided the perfect end to a good day. He took bread from the freezer, also homemade. "Doesn't seem to mind a stay in the freezer so when I bake I bake several."

With everyone well fed, including Bigcat, and everything cleaned up and back in proper order, they all went back to the fire. It had reduced itself to a bed of red coals and Tog poked at them then added a chunk of wood. He settled into his chair and retrieved a long stemmed pipe from a table behind him. The same one that Jonathan had seen on the porch or one just like it. "I've got others if you'd like one." Tog held the pipe up and gestured to Jonathan.

"I think I'm good, thanks." Jonathan wondered if Tog intended to pick up where he had left off. Bigcat curled himself into a ball in the center of the rug and appeared set for the night. It wasn't too long before Tog finished his pipe and at the fireplace he leaned down and scraped the bowl clean. The fire had calmed and small flames darted and licked what remained of the wood Tog had added. Tog adjusted the screen tight to the bricks and turned and as he passed he placed his hand on Jonathan's shoulder.

"A good day my friend, coffee's on at 5:30." Tog said nothing more and headed to the stairway. Jonathan sat until the fire had settled to a safe bed of glowing coals then checked the screen and gave Bigcat a pat before heading to his room.

He undressed and hung his clothes on the bed post and then emptied his bag from the morning's shopping. He set each item in a row on the bed like a child getting ready for the first day of school. The day had been busy but Jonathan repeatedly thought about Tog's calling him a shadow man. He took his notebook and with the two pillows propped against the head board he slipped the pencil from the notebook and opened it. Flipping to a new page he wrote: *May 19* and under that *Shadow Man.* He made notes of what he had bought, the $100.00 that Tog gave him, his return trip to Greta's, what they accomplished and while he did this he looked at his left hand and he wrote *Lara and...*he stopped and then wrote *Lara* again, but nothing came. Jonathan flipped to a new page and listed the things he knew about and things he knew how to do that had come up that day.

That night, in the light of the full moon, from his window Jonathan could see up to the edge of the tree line and around to the east toward the front of the house. He pulled the curtains to, but then opened them again and went to lie on the bed. From his position on the bed he could see the night's shadows pass under the moon's shine and he thought how Tog had seen far beyond anything he had said. He wondered if Tog would delve into the shadows or wait for Jonathan to emerge from them. With the covers pulled to his neck and his hands resting across his stomach he fell asleep.

When the smell of coffee woke him and he heard rustling sounds from the kitchen, it surprised Jonathan; certain he had just fallen asleep. He got up and took a short shower, shaved and then dressed in some of his new clothes. The pants were fine, the belt perfect, but the shirts needed a little blousing to tuck in neatly. He brushed his hair in front of the bureau and stood pleased with what he saw. "I guess it looks like me," he thought and then with hat in hand he went out to the kitchen.

"Waffles?" Tog said without turning. I wasn't a question as much as a statement of fact. Tog whipped batter in a large gold bowl and what looked like an antique griddle sat to his left on the counter. Bigcat snaked his way back and forth between Tog's legs either thanking him for his breakfast or waiting for it.

Tog poured coffee into a white mug and turned to hand it to Jonathan. "You up for a half day? Around noon I'm headed to Lincoln to see Mom. You're welcome to come along if you'd like." Turning back to the stove he poured batter into the griddle and breakfast got underway.

117

Jonathan pulled a chair out and sat at the table. Bigcat left Tog and came over and wound himself around Jonathan's feet. "Half a day's good for me. Maybe I'll know enough of what's next to keep going when you head out."

Tog lifted the lid of the griddle to check the waffles. "You could be his best friend if you poured him more milk." Jonathan got up and went to the refrigerator almost stumbling over Bigfoot as he turned to race ahead of him.

Tog lifted one waffle from the griddle and set it on a plate. He brushed butter onto the griddle and poured in more batter. "Get it while it's hot." Tog handed the plate to Jonathan as he passed.

They were finishing the clean-up when the cat headed toward the door and then in a minute the sound of tires on the crushed gravel could be heard from the front drive. Tog headed toward the door. "And a good Sunday morning to you." He swung the door wide and Becky, Greta's granddaughter stepped in. "Headed to work?"

"Errands first, not going in 'til noon. You didn't tell me you were making waffles." Becky set a big tote bag on the floor and gave Tog a hug.

"You didn't tell me you were coming—coffee?"

"Great, I brought those maps to show you," Becky looked past Tog and saw Jonathan coming from the kitchen, "Good morning, Jonathan right? I remember Brad calling you Jonathan."

"Good morning. How do you want your coffee?" Jonathan

smiled and waited at the doorway.

"Black is fine, thanks." Tog and Becky went into the map room and Tog cleared a space. Becky pulled the chair up and took out several rolled maps and began to lay them out on the table. When Jonathan came in with the coffee Tog stood behind Becky leaning forward and looking over her shoulder. Becky looked up at Tog, "Not bad for $42.00."

Tog stood up and to the side and gave Becky a thumbs up. "You did well. Take a look at this Jonathan, it's Maliseet land. They were sometimes called the St. John Indians, but they called themselves 'Wulustukeg'. They occupied the eastern boundaries of the US and Canada. This is a good one." Jonathan stepped in to look more closely at the map that Becky held open.

"Greta running the show alone this morning?" Tog leaned over Becky and smoothed a corner of the map.

"She's there. She called late yesterday and said if the stove parts came to hang a sign: "Open at Noon." Parts came late afternoon and she's got the service people coming early this morning." Becky spun the chair around to face Tog and Jonathan. "So what are you two up to? Looks like you've got a good start on the new mini-barn?"

"Good day yesterday. He knows a thing or two about building and tools too. Probably get organized for tomorrow and then head down to Lincoln to see Mom."

"How's she doing?" Becky got up and swung the chair back under the edge of the table.

119

"Doing well, no change, but she seems happy." Tog held his coffee cup up, "More?"

"Sure, I'll get it," Becky headed into the kitchen.

Jonathan followed and rinsed his cup at the sink. Becky and Tog were quite involved in their maps and he didn't want to be a fifth wheel. "I'm going to head outside. Tog came from the map room and he passed him in the hallway.

Outside Jonathan took a deep breath and walked down past the barn site to where the fence line left the road. He followed the fence to the tree line and then crossed along the top of a small rise and looked back at his window where he had watched shadows the night before. The aloneness that ached inside of him and a yearning would not come into focus. He walked slowly, wondering not only who he was, but what kind of man was he trying to recover. The morning air felt crisp and as he walked he saw where the ground had been pawed and turned where the sheep and Lamas had stood and bits of fur were stuck to the bark of a tall ash tree. Jonathan made his way across and turned to come down behind the barn site. As he came across the pasture, Becky and Tog were saying good bye at her car. Not just any car, but a dark blue, restored, 1967 Ford Mustang. Jonathan waved as Becky backed around and drove out Tog's road taking care to miss the many ruts and holes.

"How's everything look?" Tog came toward Jonathan who had stopped where they intended to work.

"Looks good, pretty much as we left it."

"See any tracks out there?" Tog turned and looked past the house up toward the rise at the tree line.

"Nope, only saw the sheep's and the llamas. I saw lot of pawing and scratching in the ground."

"Yeah, they seem to like hanging out there nights, especially with the full moon. They'll be edgy tonight with the eclipse and all."

"Eclipse?"

"Solar eclipse, after sundown so we won't see it, but the animals will know." Tog walked over to the tarp and lifted one corner. He reached under and pulled out the gas can. "Let's gas up the Polaris in case we want it tomorrow."

Jonathan followed Tog to the green ATV parked alongside the truck and Jeep. Tog didn't pour gas into the machine, but instead leaned in and started it and set the gas can in back. "Hop aboard." Tog backed the machine around and headed down the drive. Across from the broken fence line, Tog pulled up next to a stockade enclosure that was eight by eight and six feet high. He parked close to the fencing and shut the machine off. "Don't like having gasoline up next to the house or the feed, plus its easy here for deliveries." A long 'L' shaped piece of steel hung on the gate and fell through two guides into a pipe set into the ground. Tog pulled it up and one section of fence swung open and inside a tank sat cradled in a frame with a hose attached and a crank handle. "Grab that hose," Tog twisted the gas cap off and then reached in back for the gas can.

Back at the house, Tog parked the Polaris to the far side of the pick-up truck and shut it off. "I never know when I might need this so I like to keep it at the ready." Jonathan reached in and took the gas can and headed over to the tarp. Think I'll head down; sure you don't want to go? I'd enjoy the company." Tog stood with his hands stuffed in his back pockets.

"Actually, I think I will go thanks."

By ten o'clock Bigcat, the house and all chores were tended to and Tog and Jonathan headed down the drive in the Jeep. Soon after they intersected the South Oakley Road Tog turned off onto the road Brad had brought Jonathan in on. Tog slowed as he passed Kitty's house and blew the horn twice and continued on. "Brad's due in late today or tomorrow morning, I think he's taking some time this trip."

At Linneus they turned onto 2A south toward Lincoln. The late May sun was bright, but early May held onto Maine's northern chill. Jonathan sat watching out the window and when they passed by Greta's some trucks had pulled in to get off the road or were waiting, no doubt the closed 'til noon sign had gone out over the air. South of Greta's on the left, Tog pulled off into Shady Pines. "Great sandwiches here—come on we'll get a couple for down the road." Tog opened his door and Jonathan followed. Outside, the late morning sun had warmed the day considerably. A tall young man with sandy hair and multiple ear piercings carried a bundle of Sunday papers in from the wire rack on the porch. Tog grabbed the door and held it. Inside the young man set the newspapers on top of a small pile to the right of the register.

"Phil and Bev take the day off?" Tog swung a paper around and glanced at the headlines.

"They headed down to Bangor. It's Bev's Dads 65th and they're having a big party. I'm covering for them."

"Well, I'm guessing you know how to run that grill." Tog smiled and turned the paper back around.

With sandwiches wrapped in tin foil, two drinks and a bag of chips, Tog and Jonathan headed back to the truck. Jonathan recognized much of the road as they headed south to Lincoln, a reverse of his ride with Brad. The light Sunday traffic more often than not consisted of trucks. Jonathan spotted the turn into Haskell's cabin and farther down the tote road off to the right where he had found himself.

"Ever been to Lincoln?" Tog glances over at Jonathan and then back at the road. "Nice little town, not too far so getting down to see Mom even in the bad weather isn't too bad." Jonathan watches the hardwoods flash by on the left and looks at the high ledges on the other.

"Come to think of it, you've never said where you're from." Tog says this acting as though it just occurred to him. "So?" Tog adds.

Jonathan looks out to his right where a break in the ledge reveals a long view to the west. In front, the road, like an endless black ribbon with a dashed line down the center, runs straight for as far as you can see. He looks at Tog who is resting his right hand on the steering wheel and looking partly at

Jonathan and partly at the road.

"You're right." Jonathan shifts in his seat and faces more toward Tog. "Where I'm from is about as clear to me as where I am going. The truth is, I don't know." He looked directly at Tog, whose position had not changed. "I'm Jonathan only because I gave myself that name. I gave it to myself the day before I met Brad. I know myself as well as you do, we all met about the same time." Jonathan looked out through the windshield and then back at Tog.

"And the writing project?" Tog asks and then adds. "Hell I never bought that in the first place."

"Actually made that up. "It's turning into an interesting story though. Like you said, I'm just a shadow of a man, an unknown man and I'm trying to find him." With this, Jonathan looked directly at Tog and then back to the front. Tog turned toward Jonathan and reached across and touched Jonathan's shoulder.

"A shadow leads us, follows us, or stands off to the side and exists because of the man, but the man has body and spirit. The shadow reveals nothing, but the man does. We'll find you my friend." And then he turned back to look ahead.

The rest of the drive to Lincoln flew by as Jonathan told Tog the story as he knew it. Tog listened and other than a couple of questions said nothing. When they pulled into a small park in Lincoln to have their sandwiches, Jonathan felt renewed and free as though an enormous weight had been lifted. In one way he felt more like someone than he had before. The park nestled at the base of a small hill and wide walks led in several directions, one to The Lake Terrace Assisted Living facility. "You can drive right? Take the Jeep, there're some shops down that way," Tog pointed to Jonathan's right. "I'll be about an hour, meet me back here or stay here if you want. Not much fun inside unless your mom's there." Tog got out of the Jeep and headed toward the path that wound up through a well maintained garden. He turned and came back as Jonathan walked in front of the Jeep. He reached into his pocket and from his wallet he took three twenties and handed them to Jonathan. "Just in case." Tog turned before Jonathan could protest. From the path Tog called back, "Yesterday we had a good day—a long one, you're worth at least $15.00 an hour. Careful, I don't think you've got a license."

The idea of driving Tog's Jeep without a license intrigued Jonathan, a bit uncertain, but the adventure seemed worth it. Apparently he had done it before; he shifted the gears as though he owned the vehicle. He pulled out and drove down Taylor Street until he intersected what seemed to be a main street and then parked along the road near the entrance to a motel, deciding not to push his luck. A number of quaint shops lined the other side of the road, a hardware store, an insurance office, and what looked like a closed down political office. Jonathan locked the Jeep and crossed the street. He went into a bookstore that shared its space with a pharmacy. It had the newest arrivals in paperback, a wide selection of newspapers and magazines and a soda counter that stretched along one wall with high stools in front. On another wall an assortment of office supplies able to meet anyone's need. Jonathan glanced at the newspapers looking for anything that might suggest someone looking for him. The papers were a collection of local weekly's stacked next to a pile of The Maine Sunday Telegram. He found nothing too shocking and certainly nothing about him. He flipped through several paperbacks then went out. Attached to the brick front of the buildings a large bulletin board announced upcoming events, cats available for adoption, cars, trucks and snowmobiles for sale, and a large number of boats, canoes and other watercraft. A missing dog poster with a picture of a little girl holding a young dog that said. "Have you seen Ralph? We want him to come home. Please call." He smiled. Shouldn't there be a poster that said "Have you seen Jonathan? We want him to come home. Please call." He quickly reminded himself he was only Jonathan because he said so. A store that had what looked like, quality clothes—sporty but conservative sat back in a recess in the brick façade forming extended right angled front windows. A large display of hats caught Jonathan's attention. A real estate office closed on Sunday sat sandwiched between the clothing store and a small café called *The Salt 'n Pepper*. Jonathan stepped in to look at the hats.

The impressive display of hats presented a wide-ranging selection. A young woman who reminded Jonathan of Brad's daughter Kitty, only younger and shorter, came over and offered help. Jonathan had no plans to buy a hat and didn't need help, but the two of them had fun selecting hats she thought looked good on him. They tried several hats and as Jonathan adjusted each one the young girl would smile or frown and finally she held her thumb in the air and said "Awesome!" When Jonathan stepped out of the store he was wearing a medium brown hat made by Stetson and a good a part of Tog's sixty dollars was gone. He adjusted the hat on his brow and set the back into place and then without thinking ran his thumb and forefinger along the brim, felt good, natural. He glanced at his watch and decided he better head back to the Jeep. To his left as he came out two women came from the *Salt 'n Pepper* café. They turned one way and Jonathan the other. Jonathan stopped and turned back and watched as they walked, a mother and daughter out to lunch he thought to himself. Jonathan headed up the street and then turned again, and saw them round the corner at the end of the block.

When Jonathan got back to the Jeep he pulled into the motel on the right to turn around and headed back out. He waited while a car turned in from the road. He shielded his eyes from the bright afternoon sun as it passed and in the glare the driver's face was obscured in a halo of light. Jonathan thought, though hard to see, that it was the woman he saw coming from the café with her mother. He looked back and then pulled out and headed back to the park to meet Tog. He drove with his right hand resting on the steering wheel and with his thumb he rubbed the ring finger on his left hand.

At the park, Jonathan did not wait long before Tog came

down the path. Jonathan stood in front of the Jeep leaning back against the hood.

"Very nice, it's you for sure." Tog caught the keys that Jonathan tossed him. "Any problem driving?"

"Nope, whatever I drove it must have had a clutch. Seemed natural."

## CHAPTER TWELVE
### *... just doing their thing*

"I can't help but wonder if whoever did this to me and left me in the woods, might come back to finish what they started." Jonathan sat looking across at Tog. "...I mean they must have robbed me or something. I didn't have a wallet or anything else, just the few things I told you about."

"You said they didn't hurt you, just the irritation on your face."

"I'm guessing that has something to do with my not knowing who I am. It's like a rash, a reaction to something. Otherwise, I didn't seem to be hurt at all, can't figure it out."

"There must be people looking for you. You said you were married. How do you know?"

Jonathan held up his left hand and showed Tog the mark where a ring had been. "I feared that if I revealed myself right away the wrong people might find me before the right ones do and..."

"We'll make sure that doesn't happen." Tog interrupted.

"...and," Jonathan continued,   "...what if ...what if what or who I was, wasn't good. What if I wasn't a good person, if my life wasn't good, I mean, I've got to know, but it's scary."

"E.L. Doctorow once said about writing, that it's a lot like driving on a highway at night when you can only see as far as your headlights shine, but you could make the whole trip that way. I think life is like that: we can only see so far ahead at any time. You'll be fine; we'll take it one step at a time. If you reach out for a part of anything you can't help but be attached to the whole. Not exactly my words, but a paraphrase of John Muir's, a man much grander than me. Hell, if you don't like what you find, you seem to be pretty handy to have around."

When they turned off at Linneus, Tog took the back road, swung by Kitty's and blew the horn as they passed. Afternoon clouds were chasing the sun westward and there was a cooler feel, almost stormy look as the fast moving clouds shuttered the sunlight.

Where the road wasn't smooth Tog steered the Jeep onto the side to avoid the bigger potholes. When the house came into view and they crested a small rise opposite where the gas tank enclosure stood, Tog slammed on the brakes and brought the Jeep to a dust spraying stop. Jonathan braced himself with his hands on the dash and before he could say anything, Tog leaped from the Jeep and stood half crouched staring toward the house. Jonathan climbed out as Tog turned to come back.

Tog reached behind the seats, threw a blanket to the side and grabbed a rifle nestled there with a shovel and from a box he took a handful of rounds.

"Come on, stay behind me. Coyote!" Tog slid the bolt back, fed four rounds into the rifle and chambered one." He moved in front of the Jeep and then out and around the gas tank enclosure. Crouching low, he began to stalk forward through the grass toward the house, approaching from the back side of the barn under construction. He stopped every few steps and then moved forward. When he stopped and kneeled. Jonathan did the same. Tog settled the rifles butt into his shoulder and released the safety. Jonathan looked toward the house, following the line of Tog's rifle, but saw nothing. Tog held this position and then he fired and worked the bolt. In the distance Jonathan heard a yelping sound and saw one coyote run from the field toward the road. Tog fired again and it fell. Then to the left a large black bear rose from the underbrush. Tog swung the rifle and fired as the bear rose on his haunches and turned. Tog fired again and the bear spun, but ran erratically toward the tree-line behind the house. The bear, no doubt had been waiting to steal the coyotes kill. An opportunist at heart the bear, with an early spring hunger, would welcome an easy meal.

"Get the Jeep!" Tog called back to Jonathan and then he started down to where the bear spun away. By the time Jonathan got to the Jeep and drove it down the road, Tog had reached the spot where the bear had come out and had kneeled on the side of the road looking at the grass and dirt. In the gravel on the road, Jonathan could see a trail of blood where the bear had crossed. Tog stood up and looked back toward the pasture. The two coyote lay dead in the grass and not far two sheep lay with their necks ripped open. One had been partially eaten. Tog continued walking toward the house and Jonathan watched. He looked at the two sheep and then the coyotes and then went back to the Jeep. When he pulled the Jeep into place, Tog stood at the back of the Polaris. He came to the Jeep and retrieved the shovel from the back.

"There's a pickaxe under the tarp. We need to bury them, can't leave them exposed out there in the night. Then we'll have to find that bear. She's hurt, it's not fair." Tog set the shovel in the back of the Polaris and started it up. Jonathan got the pickaxe and met Tog as he came by.

Tog took some burlap sacks from a box in the bed of the Polaris and spread them out. He and Jonathan, each taking two legs, loaded the sheep and coyotes into the bed. The Coyotes were long and lean, but otherwise small. The sheep were good size. They drove to a spot far out and away from the house beyond the barn and buried the animals together, separated only by the burlap bag that Tog threw over the coyote before laying the sheep in. Back at the kill site, Tog used the shovel to scrape the blood and other remains into the dirt. When he pulled the Polaris in next to the Jeep he took the rifle and headed toward the porch. "Set that pick ax and shovel off to the side; I'll have to wash them off."

Jonathan caught up to Tog on the porch. "Why didn't the llamas come down?" He asked.

"Not sure, maybe the bear, maybe the eclipse. Everything's jumpy."

"Sorry about your sheep."

"It's part of it. The coyote are just doing their thing. This used to be their land, but they were driven off. Every time someone is driven off their land and they come back they're painted as the bad guy. They're not bad, it's their land." Tog shook his head slightly and then looked out toward the road. "The bear, she heard the commotion and knew there might be a free meal. Otherwise she'd have stuck to whatever she could find. Meat's not her first choice. She's hurt and angry now— more dangerous than ever. She'll hunker down in the thick stuff. It's too risky looking for her in the dark. We'll head out at first light." When they walked into the house Bigcat lay curled in the center of the rug. Either he didn't care or already knew what had happened.

◊

Jonathan and Tog sat while the adrenaline settled. Outside the evening draped the fields darker than usual. Tog got up and as he passed into the hallway, he turned back toward Jonathan" I'm gonna pour a glass of wine and then we can figure out what's for dinner. I've got other stuff too if you want it."

"Wine will be fine. I have no idea what I drank or what I

drink or even if I did."

"We'll work on that my friend," Tog said as he came in with the wine. "The surprises should be interesting, maybe even fun."

"I think interesting may be an understatement."

In the kitchen, Tog and Jonathan worked together making a tossed salad and rescuing the left over spaghetti and meatballs and slicing more of Tog's bread. The meal tasted as good the second time around as it did the first, if not better,

"Sorry, I got so wrapped up in myself and never asked how your Mom was."

"My friend, being wrapped up in yourself is hardly something to apologize for. Especially given that self is a bit illusive. I can only guess how dark these past days have been. How alone and frightening it must have been. You are not alone now. We will shine light on that darkness and find you." Tog turned toward Jonathan and tossed his dish towel onto the counter. "Brad's coming in sometime tomorrow. We'll put our heads together and figure out a plan. Not too fast, though, you've still got a barn to build. We'll take care of the bear in the morning and then get back at it.

"Things don't change with Mother. She is fine, happy, there and not much else. Each time I'm certain I'm used to it, but the truth is I brace myself for it each visit. She worked hard. Dad's death left her as a young mother with twins to raise, two who got into their share of trouble, it couldn't't have been easy. I think she wore out early." Tog ran his fingers through his hair and pulled down on the braid in back. "After my brother died it got very quiet—a lot of sadness—Mother had been broken."

Tog stopped abruptly and Jonathan did not persist. Jonathan felt certain that not only his mother had been broken and like himself, Tog too had darkness and shadows.

# CHAPTER THIRTEEN
*Special delivery*

Brad Stillman shifted through the gears until the big ten wheeler got up to highway speed. It was not a business stop at Bangor International airport–no load to drop off and no load to pick up, just a special surprise package for Kitty, Daniel and Olivia. Through a number of phone calls, Kitty's husband Dan had tracked Brad down and together they planned a surprise arrival intended to excite everyone. The flight's arrival had been scheduled for two A.M., but an inevitable delay got it there closer to four. With Dan's gear stowed and a hug that kept repeating itself finally put to rest, they headed home. Normally it would be a two hour ride plus the time to get to Kitty's, but Brad anticipated a quicker trip at that hour of the morning. Sandwiches and drinks bought at the airport were spread out on the center console and seamless stories let the miles fall fast behind. The sandwiches would hold them over until they got to Greta's where the welcoming home would begin, but they both welcomed a pit stop at Shady Pines.

Brad downshifted several times as he approached and the deep throated growl of the engine slowed the vehicle. He eased the big rig off the road, in front but past the pumps. Phil, as usual, had gotten up and at it early, opening up for the beginning of a new week. Bev had her own chores, up early too never wanting to miss coffee time that she and Phil had come to mark as the most important time of the day, a respite before reality shoveled in whatever the day might bring. Phil kneeled at the pump's island restocking a wire stand with quart containers of motor oil and another with windshield washer in gallon jugs. He looked up and when he saw the dark green truck and gold lettering, gave an emphatic wave to Brad.

When Dan stepped out of the cab and swung down to the ground, Phil had returned to stacking supplies. Dan walked over and stood behind Phil and waited. When Phil stood up expecting Brad, Dan threw his arms around him and gave him a big bear hug lifting him off the ground.

"I'll be damned," Phil gasped for a breath. "Man it is good to see you. Welcome home Marine, Semper Fi!" The two men hugged again and then the three of them walked into the store. "Hey Bev, look what I found."

Bev came from around the corner tying an apron around her waist and looked up. At first she did not speak and then she came around the counter and Dan met her half way and lifted her into his arms. "Does Kitty know?"

"Nope, only Uncle Brad and Uncle Sam, big surprise." Bev was Kitty's cousin, but they might as well have been born sisters.

"You guys must be hungry, what can I get for you?" Phil stood holding a large spatula at the ready.

"Actually we're good, just needed a pit stop if it's okay." Dan, having lowered Bev to the floor had already headed to the restroom. Phil moved behind the counter and set to straightening things up including moving the newspapers left over from Sunday. Brad caught a small stack of papers that had stuck themselves to the bottom of the newspapers and set them back on the counter. The top page, had the lower half torn off and a stain from a coffee spill. Something caught Brad's attention and he picked it up and looked at it. It had two pictures of the same man, one with and one without a hat. Along the top it said:

"Have you seen this man?" Under the picture where the tear began part of something was missing but what remained said: "...y call himself Jonathan." The rest of the flier was gone. Phil turned to prep the grill and Dan came from the restroom and stopped to talk to Bev. Brad looked at the flier again and then at the bulletin board looking for another.

"Phil," Brad said with a darting glance toward Dan and Bev. "What's this?" He held the flier for Phil to see. Phil half-turned and then went back to the grill.

"Oh, something Chief Vaillancourt from up to Pine Creek

dropped off, old news now, I think."

Brad folded the flier and put it in his shirt pocket and walked past Bev and Dan to the restroom. When Brad came out he slapped his son-in-law on the shoulder and headed to the front of the store. "Ready to saddle up, Marine?"

"So," Phil called from the grill, "big party?"

"Nope, little one, you know me and parties."

Brad and Dan thanked Phil and Bev, said good-bye and headed out to the truck. Back on the highway Brad was quiet, tired for sure.   Anxious to get to Greta's and see what she might know, Brad wondered what he had done, put his friend Tog in danger? Who was this man Jonathan and why were the police looking for him?

When Brad rounded the last curve that brought Greta's into sight it surprised him to see the parking lot empty at that hour in the morning. Usually parking came at a premium as fresh coffee and breakfast beckoned truckers in. He began down shifting and a rumble came from the engine as it slowed the big rig. When Brad pulled into the empty gravel parking area he saw the big sign affixed to the front Door: "OPEN AT NOON!"  A gas company truck angled to the side and Greta's blue Ranger sat tucked up in front of it. Lights could be seen in the kitchen but not in front and Brad eased the truck to a stop.

"Looks like breakfast may be on hold.  Greta must have a stove problem." Brad opened his door and, swinging on the large chrome assist handle, dropped himself to the gravel. Dan got out and met him as he came around in front of the truck.

The back door had been propped open and Greta could be heard talking with someone inside. "Road bandits coming in," Brad called as he opened the screen door. Greta looked up from where she stood watching a thin young man work at the stove top. She looked past Brad and saw Dan as he came from behind.

"Lord have mercy on this old soul." Greta threw her arms around Dan and they become one in a swinging and swirling hug. "I'm guessing Kitty doesn't know."

Brad had moved off to the side and the serviceman paused and looked up. "Nope, picked him up in Bangor, my surprise." Brad, more than a little anxious to ask Greta about the flier impatiently waited until Greta and Dan released each other and stood with arms around each other's waists.

"Coffee is on out front and there is a batch of doughnuts and bagels, but nothing else 'til Ryan gets things cooking again."

"Coffee's good for me, "Dan turned and headed toward the swinging doors. "Coffee, Brad?"

"And a doughnut—was expecting eggs and sausage..."Brad reached into his shirt pocket and pulled out the flier from Daggett's. He unfolded the flier and handed it to Greta. "Know anything about this."

Greta studied the flier and shook her head. "Nope, haven't seen it. Where'd this come from?"

"I found it at Daggett's. Phil said Anne Vaillancourt from Pine Creek came up through passing them out.

"Greta," the service man called from the stove, "where's that new burner assembly?"

"Oh, sorry out on the counter behind the cash register. I'll get it."

"I'll get it." the young man disappeared through the swinging doors, holding them as Dan came through with two coffees. He found the box of parts where Becky had set it on top of mail and other papers.

Brad folded the flier and gave Greta a sharp quick nod. "You look pretty busy and I need to get this surprise package delivered. Then I'm headed up to check on Tog. I'll call." Before Greta could say anything Brad had turned toward the door. Dan balanced his coffee in one hand and gave Greta a one armed hug. "I'll be down," Dan turned and followed Brad. The gas man returned with the burner assembly and a plastic bag of fittings.

Brad couldn't shake his concern for Tog, but tried to sound upbeat as they neared Kitty's. This isn't how he expected the morning to turn out, but he wasn't going to let the surprise and excitement for others be stolen. Not far up the road he passed Becky coming from the other direction. She held her hand out in a high wave and Brad pulled down on the air horn cord. "Becky, she must be headed in for the noon opening. Things must be in full swing at your house." Brad sipped coffee as he negotiated the turns that would take them home to Kitty, Daniel, and Olivia. Dan stirred in his seat unable to contain his own excitement. When they pulled off and Brad eased the truck into its designated spot, Kitty was heading into the house from the yard. She stopped and turned to wave and looked down quick as Daniel pushed by and Olivia twined herself around Kitty's legs wrapping her arms around her mother's thigh, Dan slid down in the seat out of sight. Brad swung down and came around the back of the truck and scooped Daniel up as he came running to him. They walked together up alongside the length of the truck until they reached the other door. Kitty had picked up Olivia and had walked halfway to the truck when the door opened and Dan stepped down. Daniel, pulling and twisting Brad's hat and did not see his father step down. Kitty stopped and squeezed Olivia tight to her.

"Howdy ma'am, got room for a travelling man?"

"I think we can make room," Kitty handed Olivia to Dan who came toward them with outstretched arms. Daniel turned from Brad and seeing his father, squirmed loose almost falling out of Brad's grasp.

"Daddy, Daddy!" Brad lowered him to the ground where his little legs were running before they touched the gravel. Daniel encircled his father's legs with his little arms and Dan leaned down and scooped him up adjusting Olivia to one side. Kitty wrapped her arms around all three of them. Brad leaned back against his truck and watched content the surprise package had been properly delivered.

"I'm gonna give you kids some time. I want to take a quick ride up and check in with Tog." Dan had lowered Daniel to the ground but held Olivia in his arms, Kitty had her arms around

Dan's waist and Daniel jumped and popped in front. They smiled at Brad and walked toward the house.

Brad went around to Kitty's pick-up and when he backed out he pulled up the road probably a little faster than he should have. Hearing gravel spit back from under the tires, Dan glanced back from the porch.

# CHAPTER FOURTEEN
*Unfinished business*

Jonathan woke and grasped at images that dissolved as fast as he saw them and for a minute he sat uncertain where he was. The familiar smell of coffee, usually something he caused not something he woke to, but then the fog cleared and the events of the day before came clear. On the dresser his new hat sat as though it had always been there. He threw the covers back and slid from the edge of the bed and opened the door. He could hear Tog in the kitchen murmuring, no doubt an intimate morning conversation with Bigcat. It was earlier than usual and he expected Tog wanted to get to the bear as quickly as possible. Jonathan went to the bathroom and splashed water on his face and ran his wet fingers through his hair, dressed quickly, grabbed his hat and went to the kitchen. Tog had left the kitchen, but Jonathan heard him coming from the map room. Jonathan turned after pouring his coffee and Tog stood holding two rifles. "You know how to use one of these?" Tog held a lever action Winchester up.

"Looks familiar, but ...hell I don't know, let me see it." Jonathan reached out and Tog handed him the rifle. Jonathan looked at it, turned it in his hands, then slid three fingers into the lever and opened the chamber. He examined the chamber, and then worked the lever again. "I think I do," he said turning toward the window and raising the rifle to his shoulder. "Feels okay."

"Good," Tog tossed him a box of rounds. "Put some in your pocket." He reached for the rifle and leaned it against the wall with his bolt action 30.06 "Good to have, just in case. Let's eat."

After a quick breakfast and each had part of a second cup of coffee they were at the Polaris. Tog unfolded a burlap bag and spread it over the bloodied ones from the day before and laid the two rifles side by side in back.

Tog backed the Polaris out and swung out of the driveway down the road toward where the bear had crossed. The blood in the gravel, dried now to a dark crusty brown, remained visible in the early morning light. Tog turned the vehicle off the road and headed up along the broken fence line. They rocked and rolled up over uneven terrain until they reached a point where longer grass and small bushes marked the edge of the tree line. Tog stopped and set the brake but left the motor running. He walked out in front and then along the edge of the tree line, watching the ground until he came to a small opening that led into thick growth. He turned and waved to Jonathan to come up. Jonathan maneuvered over the gear shift and into the driver's seat and drove the vehicle up to where Tog stood waiting and pulled it into the edge of the trees.

"Shut it off. She went in here." Tog balanced on one knee and held blades of grass to his nose. "Still a lot of blood. She probably didn't go far before she laid down."

Tog retrieved his rifle and took four rounds from his pocket and slid them one by one into the rifle. Jonathan did the same still surprised that he knew how.

"Scared?" Tog turned to Jonathan holding his rifle in his right hand pointed toward the ground.

"Should I be?"

"Scared is good. Scared keeps you sharp and sharp keeps you alive." Tog turned and headed toward the opening into the thick woods, and Jonathan followed. The morning began cool with clear skies. The eclipse must have drawn the clouds with it and it looked like what should be a good day. They moved slowly in part because of the thick growth and in part because Tog periodically knelt to part the leaves and debris on the ground.

"If she's hit hard the trail will be straight. She'll know where she's going and will back into a hole or a thicket to die. If she's not hit hard the trail will meander." Tog stood up and turned to Jonathan. "Stay back a little. The blood may disappear. Fat and debris clogs the wound."

Tog moved forward parting branches and ducking as he

147

made his way through thick growth. He turned and Jonathan had dropped back. "She's mad now, more dangerous. If you have to shoot, hit her hard and fast and keep her down."

The two men moved through the trees stepping around windfalls and climbing over rotted logs. As Tog suspected, the blood trail stopped, but he moved ahead following something that Jonathan did not quickly see.

◊

Brad drove with one wheel on the high point in the middle of the road and one wheel on the grass edge and in this way he could drive faster than in the ruts. An occasional rock or deep pot hole would jerk the wheel in his hands, but he held course and soon swung into Tog's road and past the gas tank enclosure. As he topped the last swell in the road he saw Tog's pick-up and the Jeep, but not the Polaris. He pulled up behind the Jeep and when he got out he saw the shovel and pick ax leaning against the truck. He lifted the shovel and looked at the caked dirt and blood on the blade and took a small clump in his hand, crumbled it and then held it to his nose.

He set the shovel down and went back to his truck where he folded the seat-back forward looking for anything that he might use to defend himself but found nothing. Brad didn't know what to expect, but wanted to be ready for anything. He walked toward the porch and tried the door. It was unlocked, but that was nothing unusual. He wasn't sure that Tog even knew where the keys were. Inside the house was quiet. Bigcat had curled himself into an endless curve that made it hard to determine where he began and where he ended. The smell of coffee lingered in the house and otherwise all seemed in order. If something happened here, it happened outside, he thought. Brad walked down the hall into the kitchen and then into Jonathan's room. The covers were pulled up to the pillows, but the bed had not been made and a stack of folded clothes sat at the foot of it. A small notebook set on the dresser. The same pack and walking stick Jonathan had when he picked him up were leaning in the corner. He looked around for a minute and then out the window. The sun, bright and above the roof line now crawled to the tree line. High on a swell above the rock strewn pasture, Brad caught an intermittent flash as the sun reflected off something metal. He moved from each side of the window until he could see better and realized the Polaris had been pulled into the trees up at the edge of the thick growth. He turned and paused as he passed by the notebook, but then continued toward the front of the house. He turned into the map room and saw the corner closet door partially ajar. Tog kept his rifles there and Brad wanted one. All that he found in the closet was a pump shot gun. Brad knew the gun well. It had been his father's and he had given it to Tog for safe keeping. When he lost his wife Brad eventually sold the house and everything else. Kitty's became home on one end, motels on the other and the road in between. The road wasn't anything new, but he couldn't go back to the empty house. Brad took the shot gun and a box of shells from the shelf.

At the pickup he remembered he had left his cell phone in his truck at Kitty's and Dan's. There was no time to go for help. He didn't know what had happened, but the bloodied shovel and police looking for Jonathan weren't adding up to anything that made him happy. He backed the pick up around and headed to where the fence line crossed the road. When he reached the Polaris tucked into the edge of the woods he shut off the truck and loaded shells into the shotgun. He stepped out and walked to the Polaris where he saw the bloodied burlap in the bed and smears of blood that swept across the lowered tailgate where something appeared to have been dragged across. Brad stooped to pass under a tree branch and started into the woods. He could see where the ground and branches were disturbed and every so often he stopped when he saw a brownish red splotch on the leaves or on a log. He felt his heart in his chest as he moved forward and could not shake the thought of the harm he may have brought to Tog. What has happened and what is this man Jonathan doing to his friend?

◊

Becky parked out front and made her way to the back door where the gas man finished loading tools back into his truck. Greta came through the door with something left behind and smiled at Becky as she stepped aside. Inside Becky found her apron hanging behind the door on a rack next to a large refrigerator.

"Looks like we're back in business." At the big double sink,

Greta soaped her hands and washed away the remains of her part in the repair effort.

"Passed Brad on my way in, looked like someone was riding with him."

"Sure was. He picked Dan up in Bangor. Big surprise for Kitty and the kids. He's concerned about Tog. I guess there's some flier out about that Jonathan character that has been in here with Brad and Tog. Do you know anything about that?"

"Nope, what do you mean concerned?"

"Guess the police are looking for him. Don't know much. He had a torn flier stained with coffee." Greta came from the sink toward Becky and reached back for a clean apron to replace her gas repair one.

"Did you get that envelope the Chief from Pine Creek left here?"

"What envelope?"

Becky went out through the swinging door. The opened UPS box sat on the counter and inflated plastic bags were still in it. She moved the box and found the envelope Anne Vaillancourt had left. She turned and handed it to Greta. Greta read the note on the outside and then opened the envelope. She read the flier and then handed it to Becky.

"We've got to get hold of Brad. He thinks this guy is bad, dangerous. He's worried about Tog." Greta took the handset from an old rotary wall phone and read down a list of numbers on a card taped to the wall until she found Brad's cell phone listed and then dialed the number. After many rings Brad's voice came over the line. "Brad Stillman, leave a name and number and I'll call back."

"We've gotta get up there." Greta untied her apron and tossed it on the counter.

"You better stay here in case someone calls. I'll go." Becky untied her apron and started out the door. "I'll take the flier. Should we call Kitty?"

'I will. I'll call you on your cell as soon as I find out anything."

"What about the police, Chief Vaillancourt?" Becky asked.

"I guess we should. Let's get to Brad and Tog first."

Becky headed out the door and when she started her car the full power of her restored Mustang announced itself. Gravel sprayed back and tires squealed as she fishtailed onto the pavement. Becky's cell phone rang almost before she got through the gears.

"Brad headed right up to Togs. He's in Kitty's pick up. Pick Dan up he'll go with you. Careful, Brad thinks he's walking into something terribly wrong, so no telling what's going on." Greta hung up the phone and leaned against the counter. Her age did not dull this lady's senses and she was in the moment.

With Dan on board Becky headed toward Tog's taking the road as Brad had with one wheel in the middle and the other on the side. The wide street tires slipped and swerved as she raced along the rutted road. When she pulled the Mustang into Tog's road she worked the steering wheel to correct a slide and headed toward the house. On the rise just before the gas enclosure

Dan pointed to the west. "There!"

From their vantage point Becky and Dan could see the Polaris pulled into the edge of the woods and Kitty's truck pulled up next to it. Becky came to a stop and looked up the rutted-path-excuse-for-a-road that weaved its way to the tree line.

"Shit, here goes." She shifted into first and started towards the tree-line. Her low slung frame and suspension complained as it scraped across rocks and ledge and the rear wheels fought for purchase in the grassy rutted path.

◊

Broken branches, trampled grass and disturbed ground made the path easy to follow. It meandered first left and then right and Brad moved quickly. When he stopped to listen, in the distance he heard muffled sounds of movement. He picked up his pace ducking under low branches, guarding his eyes with a raised forearm and quickly hurdled windfalls and other obstructions. Shards of sunlight cut down through the branches and sliced through the forest warming the late morning air. The blood that Brad had seen at the start of the trail had disappeared. The trail, somewhat trampled, appeared disturbed more to one side than the other as though something dragging, but not being dragged. He stopped to listen but the forest was silent. He waited and then he heard the muffled sounds of voices ahead. He could not make out what was said only a sharpness, like an order or command. Brad moved forward, heel toe quietly but quickly trying to close the gap between him and the voices. He ducked beneath a large oak that had partially fallen and hung caught in the branches of a sister tree. As he stood up he could see silhouettes ahead. One was in front of the other and the back figure was clearly holding something in his hands.

◊

Tog stopped suddenly and held his hand to the side and patted the air signaling Jonathan to stop. Jonathan stopped and held the rifle across in front of him. Tog looked back and then pointed ahead where the root side of a big windfall blocked part of the trail. Tog pointed to the left and then swung his right arm in a slow arc from the right back to the left showing Jonathan where he was going. He held up his hand which Jonathan understood to mean "Stay Put." The big man crouched and followed the arc he had made with his arm. He stepped around the root ball and his right foot sank deep into the ruptured earth and he fell with his weight rolling to the side and twisting his leg. A sudden crash came from the left, a guttural growl and the wounded black bear rose from behind the downed tree and launched herself as if from a spring board toward Tog.

Jonathan raised the Winchester to his shoulder and fired. He hit the bear high in the shoulder area at the base of the neck. The bear spun in the direction of her new wound and faced Jonathan who had chambered a second round and fired. At first he thought he had missed and then realized he had shot directly into the bear's mouth. He worked the lever on the rifle and fired again and the bear twisted and fell out of sight.

"Put it down! Put the damn gun down or I'll drop you right there." Brad stepped into the trail from behind tress that had blocked his view. "Now, drop it Jonathan or whoever the hell you are."

Jonathan held the Winchester far away from his body and slowly stooped to lay it on the ground.

"Now back away!"

"What in hell is going on?' Tog hollered from behind the fallen tree's root ball where he had pulled himself up enough to see beyond the debris that trapped him. "What the hell are you doing, Brad?"

'I've got him. Are you alright"

"My foot is caught. I messed up my ankle. Put that damn gun down and help me out of this hole. Nice shooting, Jonathan."

"Nice shooting? What the hell are you talking about?' Brad still had the shot gun aimed at Jonathan's back and Jonathan stood in a half crouched position waiting for whatever came next.

"Nice shooting. He took that bear out almost in mid-air. The damn thing had taken a real serious interest in me here in this hole."

"Bear?'

"Yes, bear! Wounded her last night while dealing with some coyote. Had to find her this morning. I saw something and worked around to her when I got sucked into a muck hole. Damn good thing he knew how that Winchester worked." Tog raised himself on one elbow but couldn't free his twisted leg from the tangled debris that held him captive.

Brad lowered the shotgun and Jonathan turned around to look at him and then went forward to help Tog. Brad stepped around the root ball and saw the bear curled in a fur ball as though sleeping then he went and together he and Jonathon freed Togs foot. It did not appear that anything was broken, but running a marathon in the near future would not be on Tog's calendar.

The crashing noise coming through the trees startled all three of them and both Jonathan and Tog reached for their rifles.

"We heard shots." Dan came into view with Becky only steps behind and they both were breathing hard. Their faces and arms were scratched from racing down the trail.

Tog settled back. "Well I'll be damned. Will you look who rode in with the cavalry!" Brad tore strips from his new shirt and using short sapling branches formed a splint for Tog's ankle and lower leg just in case. Jonathan and Dan supported Tog between them and with Brad and Becky in the lead they made their way back to the vehicles. It wasn't until after they had positioned on the Polaris that Brad turned to Jonathan and placed a hand on his shoulder. "I'm sorry, Jonathan, I thought…" Jonathan stopped him mid-sentence.

"I don't imagine it looked too good when you came through

that underbrush. Glad you didn't shoot first and ask questions later."

Jonathan drove the Polaris back to the house and Dan rode in back with Tog. Brad rode down with Becky in the Mustang. "Here, I think you should see this." Becky handed Brad the flier from Greta's." Becky negotiated a smooth path in the grass and avoided additional serious scraping or insult to the Mustang.

Back at the house, Tog presented a serious and winning argument against going to the hospital. He wasn't a big fan of doctors or hospitals and in his mind this was far too small an issue for either. With the argument at a standstill he settled into a chair where ice wrapped in towels soothed his ankle. Becky knew something from a summer as a paramedic and Jonathan, not knowing why, had useful knowledge of emergency first aid. Between the two of them with a certain amount of touching, pushing and pulling they agreed nothing had been broken and although an x-ray would be good saw no point in continuing the argument. Becky called Greta.

"Greta wants to know if she should call Chief Vaillancourt." Becky holds the phone and looks across at Tog.

"Wait." Tog said. He thought things should calm down a bit before jumping into another whole drama. Nothing would change that much overnight.

Dan called Kitty and Bigcat relished the company and flurry of activity. With everything under control, Becky and Dan got ready to leave

"I'm gonna stay up here for a bit. "Brad said as he walked with Dan and Becky out to her car. "I'll call if I'm not coming down tonight. You do still have that cell phone don't you Tog."

"In the desk drawer—turned off. Probably need to charge it." Tog gestured toward the map room where the three firearms were leaning together near the door. Becky and Dan left in the Mustang and Jonathan excused himself to get cleaned up and get a new shirt.

When Jonathan left the room Brad took the flier from his shirt pocket, unfolded it and showed it to Tog. Tog read the flier and handed it back.

"I know what he is doing and what happened. He told me yesterday. My guess is someone must be missing him and looking for him. Put that away for now .We'll figure this out, but he's a bit uneasy about it all." Tog adjusted himself in his chair and repositioned his leg on the big ottoman Becky had pulled in from the map room. "This has been an interesting day. How was your run and where'd you find Dan?"

"Bangor. Had to pry him from the arms of the greeters, but they finally let me have him and I brought him home to surprise Kitty and the grand-kids." Brad went on to explain the partial flier he had gotten at Daggett's and how all he knew was that the police were looking for Jonathan. He told Tog he had seen the bloodied shovel and then the blood in the Polaris and added up the wrong two plus two. "I came around that corner and thought he had shot you. Never saw the damn bear. Turns out a flier had been dropped at Greta's but she hadn't seen it.

Becky gave her an envelope Chief Vaillancourt had dropped off and that's when Becky and Dan joined the cavalry." Brad swung a chair around to face Tog.

"He handled that Winchester with ease. I wonder what he did, who he is." Tog laced his fingers behind his neck. "This guy is smart and a skilled carpenter too. Guess we'll get the puzzle pieces sorted out and put together. He's apprehensive about what he will find. Have to go easy—baby steps. At least now he knows he's not alone. Give Greta a call. Tell her I want to give it a day. I'll be down and we can discuss what to do next."

Jonathan came through the hallway with wet hair and brushed back and he had the second of his two new shirts on, clean pants and wearing the slippers Tog had loaned him.

"So, did Tog tell you who I am, or maybe I should say who I'm not?"

## CHAPTER FIFTEEN
*Gourmet dinner*

Brad left Jonathan in charge of Tog and headed back to Kitty and Dan's to recapture the moment he lost when he rushed off to Tog's. When he pulled the pick-up into the yard he got out and went to his truck to grab his duffle and retrieve his cell phone. Brad found Greta's number in his directory and called. He leaned against his truck and waited. The phone rang several times before it was answered.

"Becky, is Greta able to take the phone?"

"Let me check. I think so; she was hoping you'd call. How's Tog?"

"A lot of swelling, but it'll take a lot more than that to put that man down. He'll be fine. Jonathan is in charge."

"Here's Greta."

Brad explained the situation and filled in anything that Becky had not already told her. He told her that Tog wanted a day and not to make any calls until he came down. He explained a little of what he thought Togs concerns and thoughts were but he wasn't sure yet himself. Greta protested, suggesting they should call Chef Vaillancourt but in the end it was clear, right or wrong, that Tog would call the next move.

Brad's arrival back at the house went unnoticed as well it should. The real arrival, inside, and after a year plus in a war zone he had center stage. Brad finished his call and headed to the house with his duffle bag over his shoulder. Inside Dan and Kitty sat at the kitchen table, Olivia bounced on Dan's knee and Daniel carefully explained some drawings he had spread out on the table. Kitty looked up and smiled and Brad gestured toward the hall and then went down to his room at the end on the right. After a while Kitty came down and stood in his door. Brad looked up from sorting clothes from his bag into two piles–clean and dirty.

"You okay, Dad? Thanks for the surprise. Not sure how you pulled it off, but it's really great. I..." Tears rolled down Kitty's cheeks and Brad took her into his arms.

"Wasn't me. Dan called until he tracked me down and I just made sure I got to Bangor at the right time. Sorry for the little ripple when I got here."

"Dan said everything's all right. Will you fill me in later? Want to come in? Can I get you anything? Can you stay for a while?" Kitty wrapped her arm around her father's waist and walked to the kitchen with him to where the family was waiting. Kitty always asked several questions in a row and rarely waited for the answer to any and then later would ask them all over again—something she inherited from her mother.

◊

"Upstairs in the back bedroom there're two closets, check the one on the far right. There should be an old pair of adjustable crutches. My brother broke his leg when we were sophomores in high school." Jonathan went upstairs and after a while called down to Tog that there were no crutches. "Okay, in my room the flat panel door goes up to the attic, see if they are at the top of the steps."

Jonathan found the crutches leaning in a corner at the top of the steps. "Got'em," he called down. The wooden crutches adjusted to the extent that you unscrewed a wing nut on each, pulled a pin out and then replaced it in a different hole. The arm pit pads had cracked and peeled from age. "A little cleaning and some TLC and they should be good."

"Grab the blanket and a couple of pillows from my bed while you're up there. I'll probably be better off down here tonight."

Tog's room, the largest upstairs, looked out at the same view that Jonathan's did. In the corner offering a view to the east there was a large upholstered chair with a matching ottoman albeit somewhat threadbare. A floor lamp with a metal arm that swung on a steel rod set next to the chair and stood as a mast rising from a pile of books. The books formed a waterfall of shapes cascading over and across each other. A large walk in closet had its own window high in the wall and some sort of chain system opened and closed it. On the south wall, to the right of the bed, several pictures of all sizes and shapes were arranged in a random pattern. Many were of two boys, no doubt Tog and his brother. Along the top, aligned one with the other, was a matched series of a man in uniform and this Jonathan assumed to be Tog's father. Hanging scattered throughout, incredible images of a beautiful smiling woman with dark hair more often than not braided—his mother. "Anything else," Jonathan called down as he started down the stairs.

"Later. Probably need some things from the bathroom."

Jonathan set Tog's blanket and pillows from his bed on the window seat. He gathered up the large pillows and other miscellaneous clutter and stacked it on the floor to one side.

"Sorry, never got to my cleaning this week," Tog smiled as he watched Jonathan spread the blanket on top of the window seat.

"Got something I can wrap these pads with? They look a bit tired."

"Duct tape in the drawer to the right of the sink."

"That should work. I'll clean 'em up and then we can see what adjustment they need." Jonathan took the crutches and went to the kitchen. "Want anything while I'm in here?"

"If you promise not to tell, there's some Scotch in the cabinet over the Philco."

"Doubt anyone would believe a guy who doesn't even know who he is. Water?"

"Ice is good, for the Scotch and some more for the ankle too."

"So, nothing looks too strange in here—I should be able to manage breakfast in the morning." Jonathan opened the refrigerator and checked inside, and then opened cabinets. "How about a gourmet dinner of grilled cheese and tomato soup, I'm guessing you like tomato soup or you're a large stockholder with the Campbell's Company."

Jonathan found two nice glasses with a diamond design cut into the sides. He poured two Scotches and went back to the where Tog was waiting.

"Anything with it?"

"Nope, just company will be fine." Tog raised his glass. "Thanks."

Jonathan sipped his Scotch and let it roll across his tongue then looked over at Tog. "Now *that's* familiar!"

Jonathan cleaned up from the tomato soup and grilled cheese dinner which was not only good but a reminder that somehow lunch had been overlooked.  Bigcat followed Jonathan around the kitchen weaving through his legs making sure his dinner wasn't forgotten. Admitting it had been a busy day both men were happy to make it an early evening. Once he had settled Tog on the window seat Jonathan headed for his own room.

"I think Brad will be by in the morning. Maybe we can get

some work done and quit all this messing around," Tog called as Jonathan walked down the hall. Sleep came fast and hard laying claim to a day that had been full and demanding.

## CHAPTER SIXTEEN
### *Step by step*

When the children had settled for the night Brad excused himself and went to his room. Dan and Kitty made no attempt to delay the privacy. Brad got up early and had pancakes ready to go as the children woke and he encouraged them to stay quiet and let their parents sleep. Brad had forgotten how difficult that might be. The aroma of coffee and pancakes wafting through a small house is not conducive to sleep and in short order both Dan and Kitty appeared from their room. With breakfast finished, Kitty steered her father aside and took command of the clean-up. Dan went to shower and shave and Brad became an attentive audience as Daniel went to great length explaining a Lego tower and building complex that he was building with sometimes unwelcome help from Olivia. After a while Dan returned wearing jeans, a University of Maine sweatshirt and bare feet. His short cropped hair and clean shaven face made him look very much a Marine. He turned and smiled at Brad who had stretched out on the floor with Daniel inspecting the entrance to what must be the underground garage.

"I'm going into take a shower." Kitty hung the dish towel on the oven handle and turned toward the others.

"I'm headed to pick up Tog." Brad stood up and Daniel continued construction allowing Olivia to join as a participant. "He needs to take care of some business and check on the fence delivery and then we need to see Greta."

Dan settled into a recliner at the corner of the room. "Does Greta know about all that's going on, I mean with Jonathan and all?"

"Actually she's in the middle in a way. I guess The Chief from Pine Creek was at the diner with fliers looking for her the day before we came through."

"Anne Vaillancourt, she's still chief down there isn't she?"

"She is—that's right I forgot you knew her from high school."

Kitty settled on the arm of Dan's chair and put her hand on his neck. "I guess you'll get lunch at Greta's. Are you here for dinner?"

"Let me see how things are going at Tog's. I'm sure Jonathan is doing fine, but I may stay and help a bit. I'll call."

May eased itself toward June and even northern Maine warmed to the gradual change. The bright morning sun cut through the windshield and Brad slipped his sunglasses from the case, settled them over his ears and adjusted them on the bridge of his nose. Everything about the morning effervesced calm, one of those mornings with a rush of relief, not unlike after finishing a long run through unfriendly weather. Brad felt and welcomed it. It had been a tense drive from Daggett's Shady Pines and then on to Tog's that left him fearful of what he had been a part of. Looking back he felt sorry for misjudging Jonathan, but any guilt dissolved away given the bond he had with Tog. They had shared tough times through the years. It was Tog who provided the much needed sounding board through Brad's wife's illness and at her death. Brad had remained stoic through it all trying to shield Kitty from the pain of losing her mother. Inside he had been crumbling and Tog and Bigcat sat quietly until Brad was ready. They listened and caught the crumbs as they fell and helped Brad to put them back together–they were his glue.

It wasn't the first time Brad and Tog had spent endless hours together working out the pain of loss. In a similar way, Tog remained the stoic one trying to shield his mother from the pain of losing her son. Brad had not yet retired as the high school coach and had not yet started a second career driving trailer truck from Houlton down through Bangor and beyond. Brad, was young with only two years into his job when the star of the team died in his arms on the basketball court. It was long before defibrillators were positioned in schools, but even that wouldn't have helped. Wynono went down fast and hard not unlike Jonathan's bear. There had been no time to do anything. If it hadn't happened that night in the midst of a basketball game it was waiting—could have been at Saturday breakfast—there was no warning and nothing anyone could do. Brad spent days with Tog and his mother. She rallied and saw that Tog paid attention to school work and she got him off to college, but she struggled, a woman broken inside. Tog and Brad became a cross between brothers and father and son— and more.

◊

The Polaris sat backed into the barn site and Tog leaned against the tailgate with his crutches resting in the bed. Jonathan stood at the top of a tall a step ladder, marking the top plate with a tape and square. Brad pulled up alongside the site and got out.

"Well, I'm glad to see you guys have decided to get on with it." Brad stood in front of Tog and looked down at his wrapped ankle. "So, you must be the supervisor."

"This guy doesn't really need a supervisor. Pretty sure this isn't the first thing he's built."

"Morning." Jonathan called over as he came off the ladder. "I'm asking for a raise if all he's gonna do is watch."

Tog pulled his crutches from the bed of the Polaris and

hobbled over to where Jonathan had begun laying roof framing across two saw horses. "Brad's taking me down to check on the fencing. We'll probably stop at Greta's on the way back. You're welcome to come."

"I'm good here. I'll get this roof framed. Anything else I should attend to?" Jonathan stretched a cord toward the tarp that covered the tools and then pulled the tarp to the side and rolled the generator out.

Tog felt certain Jonathan would want to stay and that's how he wanted it. He needed to discuss things with Greta and decide the next step. They'd probably need to call Chief Vaillancourt sooner than later. Jonathan's fears and apprehension had calmed considerably since everyone knew his situation, but still, Tog wanted to see if they could plan a smooth way to help him on his way back without it being traumatic. It didn't seem fair to have a law enforcement vehicle swing in and dump everything in his lap. He'd no doubt get scolded, but he had been there before.

Before Tog and Brad left, Tog sent Brad in to get the cell phone from the house and he gave it to Jonathan. "I doubt you'll get any calls, but if you need to reach us Brad's number is one on speed dial, Greta is two and Kitty is three."

Jonathan waited until Brad and Tog had backed around and headed out. He waved and then started the generator, which actually went better than when Tog's first attempt to start it. He set to work on the lay out and cutting of a template for the rafters.

"I guess we need to call Chief Vaillancourt.' Tog said. "She probably will be a little miffed that we didn't call yesterday. I've got an idea that I want to run by her, but his family needs to know that he's fine and where he is." Tog took a small notebook from his shirt pocket and made some notes. "I think he's married, but I don't know if he has children or what. We never got that far and I don't think he knows, but someone is looking for him."

"Does he know what happened to him?"

"Not really. He found himself in the woods, but most everything else is gone. He has been worried that whoever dumped him might come back and then he's a little concerned about what he'll find when he finds out who he is. What kind of a man was he?"

"We'll know a lot more when we talk to Vaillancourt." Brad looked over at Tog who had gone back to his notebook.

"Keeping a diary?" Brad teased.

"No, trying to figure what's ahead. Jonathan's probably leaving soon and with this ankle, maybe I'll hold off on having more materials delivered for the barn."

"Well, Dan and I will be here for a while," Brad pulled back onto the road. "I doubt he's gonna want to watch TV all day and you can be damned sure I don't." Brad slowed as he came to the turn and Tog looked over and smiled.

At the lumber yard Tog put a hold on the fencing and then had them load the roofing materials into the pick-up. A stop at the bank and the post office and they were headed for Greta's, hopefully ahead of the lunch rush.

At Greta's there was no rhyme or reason to when it would be busy or not so to find the lot almost full late morning on a Tuesday was not altogether unusual. Tog and Brad went in through the back door and found Greta fully engaged at the stove and grille. She gestured toward a table to the side past the entry.

"Coffee's hot. Becky made two new pots. How's the ankle?" She watched as Tog leaned his crutches against the wall. Greta continued to talk from the stove and grill until orders were all out and then she went to the table where Tog and Brad sat with their coffee Brad had gotten from the front counter. She brought two plates, lunch for Brad and Tog. "You'll like this," she said. "Stir fried chicken with fresh green, yellow and red peppers, onions, and snow peas. Today's special. Soy sauce is on the table if you want it."

They talked and Tog outlined his thoughts, Brad added his and Greta offered advice and counsel. When the talking stopped a plan had been made with everyone onboard. Next they needed to call Chief Vaillancourt and get her approval and bring her into the plan. Becky came in and gave Tog a neck hug and looked down at his ankle.

"Wow, pretty interesting day." she looked over at Greta. "I clipped a couple of orders at the window."

Brad and Tog left Greta's and made one stop for groceries on the drive home.

◊

When Brad and Tog pulled past the gas enclosure they could see Jonathan on a ladder setting a rafter. "The man doesn't waste time." "Brad looked over at Tog who expressed no sign of surprise. Once they had pulled up next to the saw horses, Jonathan came from the ladder and grabbed Tog's crutches from the bed of the pick-up.

Tog slid off the seat and took the crutches from Jonathan. "Looks like you skipped your nap. Hope you went in and had lunch with Bigcat. They missed you at Greta's. Hello from Becky." Tog hobbled over to the barn and balanced on his crutches while he surveyed the work Jonathan had done.

Brad came from the truck with a box of fasteners and miscellaneous nails. The drip edge, rolls of felt and shingles were in the truck. "You sure you weren't a carpenter before I found you on the highway?" Brad slid the box up next to the wall and looked around at the project. "Dan and I are coming over in the morning. We should be able to get the roof on before afternoon tea time."

"It takes two of them to replace me, but you should be all right." Tog placed his hand on Jonathan's shoulder and then headed up toward the house. "You two coming up?"

"Let me set the last rafters. They're all cut and if Brad hands them up it'll go quick." Jonathan pulled on the air hose and stretched it toward the end of the barn.

"Be right back. Let me take the groceries in plus I had a bit too much coffee at Greta's," Brad turned and followed Tog toward the house.

## CHAPTER SEVENTEEN
*Moving forward*

Tog is sitting on the tailgate of the Polaris, his new seat of choice, with his crutches laying in the bed when the dust cloud announcing the arrival of Brad and Dan rolled up the road. Jonathan had pulled the tarp back and laid out the hose from the compressor. For whatever reason, several of the sheep and llamas lingered as if watching the final steps of something they knew had something to do with them. With June on the threshold you could feel improvement each day. The sun inching higher and with the leaves still sparse, even early morning warmed quickly.

Brad rolled to a stop off to the side and he and Dan came from the truck with tool aprons in hand.

"Now," Dan smiled as he passed Tog, "we'll get something done." He handed a greased stained bag to Tog. "Kitty made muffins."

Brad continued toward Jonathan and draped his tool belt over a sawhorse. "So, are we ready to close it in?"

Without waiting for an answer, Brad started handing pine boards to Jonathan. The boards were full length and Jonathan positioned them with adequate overhang that could be trimmed later. Brad and Dan continued laying boards in place while Jonathan started nailing. Things moved quickly with a six handed team and a one legged supervisor.

Jonathan took one end of a chalk line and Dan the other and they snapped lines to mark the overhang. Brad handed Dan the circular saw to trim the ends.

"Some trim on the gables and I think we're good to go. The drip edge is in the pick-up."

Dan headed to the pickup. "Keys are in it. Back it down here. Tog called from his perch.

Jonathan and Brad made short work of the trim boards and with the drip edge secured in place they began rolling out felt paper. Brad balanced bundles of shingles on his shoulder and climbed the ladder to lay them over the ridge. It was all too much for the sheep and llamas and as interested as they might have been they soon made their way out to the open land and up along the tree line. When he saw a short pause in the activity, Tog rustled the bag of muffins and got their attention.

"I'll hobble up and make some coffee and we can see if Kitty's muffins still measure up."

It wasn't long before Tog called down from the porch. "If you want it down there you'll have to come get it. These crutches aren't equipped for deliveries."

"We'll come up." Brad gestured to Dan and Jonathan and they all unbuckled their tool aprons and let them fall in place. Dan grabbed the bag of muffins as they passed the Polaris.

It was actually cooler inside the house than it was outside, one of the subtle signs of the season changing. A change all welcomed, man and beast alike.

Tog had efficiently transferred coffee and mugs to the table and Bigcat had come in from his rug to make sure he didn't get forgotten.

Jonathan assumed Tog had filled his friends in on most of the details and he looked at Brad and Dan. "You both okay with being characters in my story?"

"Well I'll say this, it's one hell of a story and I've heard some pretty good ones." Dan smiled taking his muffin as the plate went around.

"So, with my secret out I'm all ears to what anyone might suggest should be my next step. I'm enjoying the project and the company, but in all honesty I'd like to know who I am and where I belong.

"What's your plan?" Dan asked.

"The fence is next, I guess."

"Well, that would be one thing." Brad glanced over at Tog who stood leaning back against the counter with his wrapped ankle crossed over the other. "I meant regarding finding out who you are."

"Next is all new territory. Tog says you can only drive at

night as far as your headlights shine so I guess I'm sort of driving at night." Jonathan smiled and reached down to pat Bigcat who had settled under the table stretched across his feet. "It's all quite interesting, but I'd be lying if I didn't admit it is a bit unnerving. I probably have a family and I guess I should miss them, but none come to mind. I guess I should call the police or someone and see if I'm listed as missing. I've been shying away from that. Guess I was scared, but..." Jonathan stopped when Brad interrupted

"Well, it may be dark out there past the headlights, scary too. But you won't be walking into that darkness alone." Brad pushed back in his chair and nodded toward Tog. Dan got up and pointed toward Jonathan's room. "Bathroom."

"We're taking a break from all this." Tog spoke softly looking to where Dan had disappeared around the corner.

Brad too glanced at the hall where Dan had disappeared. "We've got a little welcome home party planned at Greta's."

On his way back, Dan picked up the coffee pot and topped off each mug. "So what do I tell Kitty? Good muffins or do I risk having to sleep in the pick-up or out the yard by saying different?"

"Well, I would think a year of combat earns you at least a nice bed and a warm body next to you. Tell her they were the best yet." Tog grabbed his crutches from where the leaned against the counter and settled them into his arm pits.

"They're the best I can remember, that's for sure." Jonathan smiled at Dan and all four men laughed.

Dan headed out first and Brad and Jonathan cleaned up the kitchen as Tog and Bigcat headed into the front room.

"So, I take it this party is a surprise." Jonathan dried each mug as Brad handed them to him.

"Hard to keep much from Dan, but one part of it will be a big surprise. With the dishes washed and back in place, Brad and Jonathan headed out.

Tog had settled in with his foot up. "I think I'll stay in. Supposed to keep this raised and I think it's telling me so."

Brad turned toward Jonathan." So we're on our own, I guess. No supervisor. I guess we'll be okay."

"He doesn't need much supervising." Tog laced his fingers behind his head and settled back in his chair.

# CHAPTER EIGHTEEN
*Party!*

W hen Brad, Jonathan and Tog arrived at Greta's they pulled into a parking lot emptier than expected. Becky's Mustang had been pulled around at the back door tucked beside Greta's Ranger. Out front one big rig had parked well past the sign and far toward the back of the lot. A white Pickup with gold lettering and other markings and lights had backed in at the far end of the building next to a green Ford Explorer, but otherwise it looked like a slow lunch hour. Brad pulled Tog's Jeep up to the building on the end nearest the back door and then went around to where Tog perched already half way out and Jonathan handed the crutches to him and then flipped the seat forward and got out. You would think he had been on the crutches for weeks if you watched Tog maneuver across the gravel lot and up the steps. Brad held the door as Tog swung into the diner. Becky had seen them pull in and met Tog at the door and checking out the wrapped ankle as Brad and Jonathan stepped behind them. Greta waved from the kitchen as Brad and Jonathan moved down to the third booth which seemed to be their favorite and Jonathan slid in facing toward the door and Brad sat opposite him. When Tog finished showing off his crutch maneuvers to Becky he came to the booth.

"I think I'll be best there," Tog gestured to Jonathan. I'm watching for someone plus it'll let me stretch my leg out a bit."

Jonathan got up and slid in next to Brad. "So, where's Dan?" Jonathan asked then looked first at the counter where a single trucker sat finishing a bowl of chowder and then toward the back room, the general store and several larger tables set up. A group of three women sat at a large round table that had been pulled forward nearer the doorway. A fourth chair had been pulled out as though they were expecting a fourth. The women talked amongst themselves and Jonathan watched for a minute feeling certain one seemed very familiar.

"Brad Stillman, now that's a name I haven't heard for quite a while." Anne said as she walked toward them. "How are you?" Jonathan looked up and saw a striking woman in a police uniform coming from the area near the kitchen door.

"Best I see you for lunch then on the road barrel assing through Pine Creek. Good to see you Chief" Brad smiled and half stood in his cramped corner of the booth.

"Sit, sit, Brad. Where's the guest of honor. Phil Daggett said he stopped down at Shady pines?"

"Coming with Kitty and the children, couldn't really keep it a surprise. Chief, I'd like you to meet my friend Togquos; he lives up a ways past Kitty and Dan's."

"Tog will do fine." Tog extended a hand to Anne Vaillancourt which she took and shook warmly.

"And this is our friend Jonathan."

Anne looked at Jonathan and smiled.

"Pleased to meet you Chief," Jonathan stood and offered his hand to Anne.

"Likewise, Jonathan, I'm very pleased to meet you." When Anne Vaillancourt left, Jonathan's eyes followed Anne as she took the fourth seat with the women in the next room. Jonathan watched as the four women talked again struck with how familiar one of the women looked. The woman to the right was partly hidden behind the door frame, but as she spoke she leaned forward glancing at Jonathan and he could see her profile. Brad unrolled the knife fork and spoon bundled in a napkin held tight with a little green paper ring. Tog watched Jonathan and stretched his leg forward as far as he could and let his ankle lean against the side of Jonathan's seat.

Jonathan turned to Tog and then to Brad. "One of those women the chief is sitting with looks very familiar." Tog turned and looked quickly toward the three women and the chief.

"Don't know 'em. Greta's reputation spreads far and wide,

probably just looking for a good lunch."

"It's coming back now." Jonathan sat forward in the booth. "In Lincoln, Sunday, I saw here coming out of a café with a younger woman after I bought my hat and then again when I turned around in a motel parking lot." Jonathan smiled content to have solved one small mystery. He leaned to one side to see past Anne's shoulder. I saw the woman on the right too. They walked past together."

Jonathan thought the woman at the corner smiled as he looked back at them and Tog leaned forward to speak, a flurry of activity as Dan and Kitty and the children came through the door interrupted everything. Daniel and Olivia jumped up on the seat of the booth behind Brad and Jonathan and reached over grabbing their grandfather around the neck.

"Boots off the seat," Kitty scolded as she took Daniels hand and directed him to a sitting position.

"I'll come over there," Brad said. Jonathan stood and slid off the seat to let Brad out and Tog, with some effort, quickly retracted his stretched out leg. After a little discussion of who was going to be on which side, Daniel and Olivia settled down with Brad between them. Dan spoke to Tog, asked about the ankle, and then said something to Kitty before going into the kitchen to speak to Greta. When Jonathan slid back onto his seat he looked again through to the other room and this time his eyes met those of the two women that he believed he had seen in Lincoln. Anne Vaillancourt watched them and the other woman sat fidgeting with her silverware wrap.

Jonathan stood up almost in slow motion and Tog sat up straight, Kitty said something to Brad and Brad turned as Jonathan moved toward the back room. From the kitchen Dan and Greta watched. Becky set the coffee pot back in place. Jonathan walked toward the table. When he reached the doorway Anne Vaillancourt looked at him. The woman to the right looked at Jonathan and smiled. The other woman from Lincoln sat motionless. The third woman continued to fidget with her silverware.

Anne Vaillancourt pushed back in her chair "Jonathan, I'd like you to meet my friends. This is Lara Andersen and her daughters Lucy and Lynn, the chief smiled and sat forward toward the table.

Jonathan stood without moving he looked first at Lucy and then at Lynn who now put her hands in her lap and looked up. "I'm pleased to…" Jonathan stopped midsentence and looked at Anne and then at Lara. "Lara?" He lifted his left hand and glanced down at it. He looked again at Anne then at Lynn and back at Lucy. Lynn did not speak, but her eyes glistened over and Lucy smiled with tightly pursed lips and when Jonathan turned toward Lara she slid a closed fist toward him and turned her hand upright and opened it. Jonathan hesitated and then reached down and took the ring from Lara's hand. He rolled it between his two fingers and then slowly slid it onto his finger. Lynn had started to cry now and Lucy looked up and said "Hi Dad." Jonathan turned from one to the other and then back to Lara. Jonathan stood unable to say more. Inside, a melting sensation spread through him, warming him. He could feel a tremble rising through him and when he spoke again his lips quivered.

"I'm sorry." Jonathan began. "You, you were standing at a door. You waved. I think I said I'd make it...quick." Jonathan turned to his left and saw that Brad and Tog had come up behind him and Dan and Kitty to their right and Greta and Becky stood to the rear. Jonathan turned toward Tog. "This is my family." Tog placed a hand on his shoulder. Jonathan stood quiet for a moment searching for the right words and then through quivering lips "And these folks," he said gesturing to those who had gathered around him and looking directly at Tog and then at Lara. "Well they've been filling in," he said smiling at Lara."

Lara stood and came around to Jonathan and wrapped her arms around him. Lucy stepped behind Anne Vaillancourt and joined in the hug and then Lynn joined too.

"This feels real good," Jonathan smiled, "but I've got to admit things are a bit blurry and I'm not real sure about ...well about anything."

"We'll work on that." Anne Vaillancourt nodded at Jonathan. "I guess we should start with your name. You're Patrick, but interestingly enough your middle name *is* Jonathan. *Patrick Jonathan Andersen.* Anne reached around to the pocket of her uniform jacket that hung on a chair and then handed Jonathan his wallet. "You may need this. I hear you've been driving without a license.

Jonathan opened the wallet and looked at his picture on his license then turned and looked at Tog. "Look at that," he said holding the wallet out for Tog to see. "Patrick Jonathan?"

"Nah, you'll always be Jonathan to me."

"Let's have a party." Greta turned and headed back to the kitchen. "See what everyone wants for drinks, Becky. Lunch is on its way."

◊

At the table Anne had switched places with Lucy and pulled a chair between herself and Lara for Jonathan. Kitty settled the children as Brad took Tog's crutches over to a spot near the wall.

Anne Vaillancourt had leaned in toward Jonathan and explained some of what they had determined over the past week. She told Jonathan about Derek Wilson and the Reverend's son. Jonathan asked an occasional question, but mostly listened. Anne tried to keep it simple and not overload Jonathan with too much too fast. She did explain about the narcotic used to subdue him and what its legitimate use was. Lara added that there is a treatment that a doctor can administer to make it all go away. "In most cases," Anne added, "both short term and long term memory is recovered." She stopped short of saying too much certain that it to be information best delivered by a doctor. "Case studies suggest you should remember everything before and after, but not the incident itself."

Jonathan revisited his blurred image of someone waving and how he said her name out load while on a trail. He asked about their cabin admitting to have no memory of it. Lucy and Lynn listened and watched Jonathan as the information seemed to settle in. Lara placed her hand on Jonathan's forearm and he looked at her and smiled. Becky came in with a tray of assorted drinks that she began distributing around the tables. Bev came with four beers that she handed to Tog, Brad, Dan, and Phil. Jonathan had ordered lemonade. Bev set two small baskets of French Fries down in front of the children.

Jonathan assumed his family must be at their cabin, but Lara explained that the trip up had been intended as a day trip and the cabin had not really been fully opened yet. "We are staying in Lincoln, Dad."

"Were you at a café there on Sunday?"

"Yes we were," Lucy looked first at her mother and then back at Jonathan." How did you know?"

"I saw you when I came out of a shop. I was there with Tog. Today I thought you looked familiar but only because I had seen you in Lincoln."

Two separate celebrations told stories, filled in blanks. Dan told some of his travel home story while Brad engaged the children. Jonathan told his own travel story relating how he met Brad and eventually Tog. He laughed when he told the story of how he explained being out on the highway in hiking boots, shorts and some borrowed equipment. "It almost sounded believable."

"Didn't fool me." Tog chimed in from the other table.

"He called me a shadow man." Jonathan glanced back at Tog.

The celebration and laughter at Dan's table competed with equal sounds of relaxed happiness from Jonathan's. Lara's caution as she asked questions melted away and they became more and more those of a concerned wife. Lucy kept pace with her mother and Lynn listened more than she talked. Jonathan anticipated the 'what's next question' and decided to head it off.

"I'll need to go back to Tog's. I don't have much, but there're some things I have to get." He wanted to go on about the projects underway, but stopped short. "Are you still in Lincoln?"

Lucy spoke first. "We are, Dad. I think it's about forty five minutes away and the cabin is maybe thirty." Lucy smiled, realizing maybe before the others that her Dad might need ...well she wasn't sure, maybe space, maybe time.

"You'll need to see a doctor, Patrick. Anne says this can all be corrected."

"Yes, but that is only a part of the whole." He looked at Anne. "I broke into a man's cabin and took some things. I borrowed them and left a note."

"That was Bret Haskell's cabin. I've already spoken to him and everything's fine. He looks forward to meeting you when you can stop by. He'll be there after Memorial Day."

Tog had gotten up and hobbled over until he was balancing

at the back of Jonathan's chair. Jonathan turned and looked up at the big man. "You put this together didn't you?"

"Well, only in part. It was actually Chief Vaillancourt who spearheaded the effort to find you. She put out a flier that we saw and Greta, Brad and I connected the dots."

"What do you want us to do, Patrick?" Lara's voice remained calm but obviously concerned.

"Don't you think you should come home, Dad?" Lynn had not spoken and she failed to conceal irritation in her voice.

"I do, Lynn and I will." Jonathan spoke softly sensing something that he couldn't pin point. "Maybe you could pick me up tomorrow here or at Tog's. I could get everything together and get organized."

Lara sat back and crossed her arms loosely. "We can follow you up to your friends and bring you home now." Lara turned when she saw Lucy look sharply at her and then toward Tog.

Tog had no question that Jonathan needed a deep long breath and some time. "Glad to get him here or even to Lincoln if you like, But I'd be proud to show you all what we've been doing if you have time tomorrow." Tog rested his hand on Jonathan's shoulder and gave it a gentle squeeze.

Again, Lynn started to say something but Lara raised her hand slightly off the table and she stopped.

"How about noon tomorrow, Mr.Togquos, can someone give us directions?" Lara spoke firmly, clearly taking control of the plan. Lucy smiled and then looked at her sister who offered a conciliatory smile.

"I can do that Mrs. Andersen or if it's easier you can meet me here and follow me up," Becky said. She smiled and leaned in to pick up plates and silverware from the table.

"That would be great. I'm sorry; I don't think we've met."

"I'm Becky, Greta's grand-daughter and Togs friend and, well, Jonathan's friend as well." Becky smiled at Jonathan and turned to set plates on a tray. "How about if we meet here about eleven?"

Lucy stood up and moved around toward Becky. "That'll be great. Thanks"

As the afternoon waned, truckers came in from the road and the counter took on an afternoon busy-ness. Greta and Becky disappeared and Bev finished clearing the party tables. Gradually the two groups merged, exchanged best wishes, congratulations and thank you-s and began to disperse. Dan, Kitty and the children were the first to leave. Brad went with them after affirming that Jonathan was in fact a licensed driver now and could legally drive back to Tog's. Phil and Bev lingered at the counter with several truckers who often stop at Shady Pines. Greta and Becky, busy in the kitchen, waved as each left. Jonathan walked with his daughters and his wife to the green Explorer parked out of sight behind Anne's pick-up. The chief said good-by and suggested they talk as soon as possible. Jonathan hugged his wife and each of his daughters, but was ready when Tog came across the gravel on his crutches.

"We'll see you tomorrow. I love you Patrick." Lara smiled as she said this and small tears left tell-tale trails on her cheek. Lynn had gotten into the back seat of the Explorer and Lucy was behind the wheel. Lara got in and rolled her window down.

"I love you too, Lara." Jonathan waved as Lucy backed the Explorer out and headed across the parking lot.

## CHAPTER NINETEEN
### *Headlights*

With Tog settled into his seat and his crutches stowed in back, Jonathan got into the driver's seat. He adjusted the seat back from where Brad had positioned it and started the engine. Then he turned the engine off. "Wow, Damn." He wrapped his arms around the steering wheel. "I need tonight, I need…"

"I know. Who wouldn't? Slow, my friend, slow and easy wins the race." Tog reached over and put his hand on Jonathan's fore arm. Jonathan had leaned over the steering wheel, but sat up straight and looked at Tog.

Jonathan restarted the engine and backed the Jeep out and when he swung around and headed out to the north, Greta and Becky were waving from the front door. They drove in silence for a while. It was early afternoon, but the sun had already been captured by the hills and tree lines and a calm dusk-ness had conquered the sky.

"I'm sure I love them. I mean, I tried to act like I did, like I knew them, but I'll tell you I haven't a clue, "Jonathan glanced toward Tog. "Lara's name–had that, but that's it."

"It's the first part. It'll come. At least we know your cabin's not far away. Get it up and running and I'm never far away. We never did find out what you did."

"Believe it or not, they say I was a teacher, a professor actually at Bowdoin."

"Hell, I pegged you for a house builder."

"Yeah, that too, I guess I built mine and damn near rebuilt Lucy's." Jonathan looked at Tog and smiled. "How about that? I guess we ought to be able to finish that barn, but I may be looking for a raise"

"We've got a fence to set, too."

"The chief said this drug I'm supposed to get brings back my memory, both short term and long term. She did say "in most cases" which she sort of added at the end." Jonathan looked over at Tog and continued. "The stuff those kids used on me is intended for surgery when you don't want the patient to remember the trauma of a procedure. It makes me wonder if I remember everything from today on and up until the attack and all that's in between is the trauma and it is forgotten. I mean, will I see you and know who I am, but not who you are?" Jonathan pushed back and with his arms fully extended drove looking straight ahead.

"No one here is about to let you forget this last week, but you can't leave the last 67 years hanging in the wind. Both are parts of who you are and we'll bring them all together."

"I wonder if I ever shot a bear." Jonathan said. He relaxed his arms and looked over at Tog "Hell, I may have been Davy Crockett in my other life for all I know."

"Right and I was Tonto riding with the Lone Ranger. Hi Yo Silver away!" At this both men began to laugh.

When Tog opened the door if Bigcat cared at all you couldn't tell. His only response was to get up and follow Tog to the kitchen because it was dinner time. Jonathan went to his room, to the bathroom he told Tog, but once inside he sat on the bed and stared at the small pile leaning in the corner that constituted his personal belongings and even most of those were borrowed or otherwise provided at the hands of others. He took his hat off, set it on the bed and smiled remembering one of the pictures that they had included on the flier–no wonder he was drawn to this hat. On the dresser, a small pile of the clothes, washed after the morning with the bear sat in waiting. Other than those and the work gloves, and what he was wearing there wasn't much to pack up and the heaviest would be his thoughts and new memories.

Tog listened, not surprised that he did not hear water running or the toilet flush. "I'm going to pour a Scotch. " He called to Jonathan. "You joining me"

Jonathan came from his room with his notebook in his hand. "Sounds good." I may be a shadow man," he said holding up his notebook, but I'm not a complete liar. I did write the story. I've chronicled everything from the day I found my way out of the woods up until this morning. Beginning middle and...well, I'll write the end now."

Neither Tog nor Jonathan felt hungry. Tog lit a small fire, not because there was any discernible chill, more for the comfort otherwise. They sipped their Scotch and revisited the day's events.

"Lara is quite lovely and your daughters are striking." Tog looked into the fire and then up at Jonathan. Jonathan smiled and nodded.

"I guess we have to pick up some legal papers in Pine Creek and Lara has spoken to a doctor who can check me out and figure what's next."

"Well, one thing's certain. You're not a drug dealer or serial killer and whatever your life is or was looks to be a successful and pleasant one."

"Funny. Can't really picture myself as a professor, I'm kind of liking the Davy Crockett image."

With more of the same the two men made their way through the evening sometimes with an edge more serious and sometimes not.

◊

In the morning, when Jonathan came from his room with Bret Haskell's pack, walking stick and battered hat and water bottles, Tog had the coffee ready and stood with one crutch leaning against the counter.

"Ankle must be better this morning. Down to one crutch?"

"Actually, much better. I'm a little surprised. I can almost put weight on it. It looks like I'll be back in the saddle in a few days or at least be able to drive again."

"Pancakes, not a question, just a statement of fact, ready soon."

"So, are we working this morning?" Jonathan set the small pack in the doorway to the hall.

"There are a few things I was hoping you'd help me with, but then we've got to put together a welcome for the ladies." There wasn't really anything to do. Brad and Dan were coming back to continue work on the barn and this time of year neither the sheep nor the llamas needed anything they couldn't take care of on their own. They straightened things out around the new barn and then took a ride around in the Polaris. The sheep and llamas had spread out and over the past week Jonathan had become used to them meandering around and accepted them as part of the picture.

The groceries Brad had carried in were all they needed for a fine lunch. Maybe more had been planned ahead than Jonathan realized. Bigcat made his daily journey from rug to kitchen and made his presence known to assure he would not be overlooked.

At 11:30 the sound of Becky's Mustang could be heard coming up the drive and behind it was the green Explorer with Lucy and Lara. Jonathan and Tog stood on the porch as they parked and then stepped down to meet them.

Lara gave Jonathan a hug and then stood back and Lucy hugged him as well. "Lynn had to get back, Dad, but she said she'll check in real soon." Lucy looked around and Lara stood close to Jonathan. Even though it was a short encounter, Jonathan felt certain that Lynn was having more difficulty with the situation than anyone else.

"One crutch, huh?" Becky gave Tog a thumbs up and headed into the house with a bag she was carrying.

"Are those lamas?" Lucy pointed toward the rise behind the new barn.

"The taller ones are. The shorter ones are sheep."

"Lucy shook her head smiled. "I can see why you and Dad hit it off so well."

"He is pretty witty." Tog said with a broad smile.

"That he is." Lara had wrapped her arm around Jonathan's lower back and was taking it all on.

At lunch, Tog related some of the history of the house and explained, with some help from Becky, the map room and their common interest in historical maps. Jonathan showed Lara and Lucy his room and Bigcat enjoyed the attention, happy to be an extended source of interest.

When appropriate good-byes had been said and after Lucy hugged Tog and thanked him and Lara shook his hand, and everyone loaded into the Explorer with Bret Haskell's gear stowed in back, Tog and Becky stood ready to say good-by.

"I'll get a phone." Jonathan smiled. "Turn yours on. I'll

call." The passenger window was rolled down and Tog reached in and Jonathan placed his hand on Tog's forearm

"Be well, my friend." Tog grasped Jonathan's hand in his and squeezed it. Lucy backed the Explorer out and started down the drive and Becky and Tog waved from the yard.

## CHAPTER TWENTY
*...but never alone!*

Almost a week had passed, a week filled with appointments, consultations and the beginnings of some treatments. Things went well, but probably not as well as many had hoped. Even though the doctor knew the drug that had been used on Jonathan, they did not know how much or exactly how. Any action to counter it was a guessing game. The treatment, if it could be called that, remained somewhat trial and error. Although responses were not negative, overall Jonathan did not experience significant change–some, but it was minor. Lara and Jonathan did return to the cabin and with little effort had it opened for the season, this in part due to a binder of lists and notes that gave directions for anyone that might use it. They were however, lists that Lara had never used because Jonathan had done it all.

Jonathan did get a new phone and almost laughed when the

technician offered to transfer his contacts. "I'm good. I think I'll start new. He wasn't surprised when he couldn't reach Tog; certain Tog's phone had been tucked back into the drawer and turned off.

Lara planned a visit to see Lucy for the Memorial Day weekend through Tuesday. Some furniture had been picked up by a reupholstering shop and Lucy had made an appointment so she and her Mom could help make the final decision between several fabric choices. Jonathan suggested it might be a great time to go up and see Tog. Lara, at first a bit reluctant, agreed, certain it couldn't be bad and was probably good.

Jonathan called Greta on Thursday and gave her his new cell number and asked her to get hold of Tog and tell him to call. She asked how things were going and Jonathan said it was a work in progress but little more. They talked for a while and Jonathan hung up promising to drive up soon.

The Friday before Memorial Day puffy cumulus clouds floated high above and the late May sun brought welcomed warmth. Lucy planned to head out after lunch and Jonathan had taken a walk out to a rock he found that looked over Turtle Pond. He told Lara about the small trail and the rock and although not sure she should or should not, Lara explained that it was at that rock that it all happened. This intrigued Jonathan and the rock became a place he visited daily.

The overhead canopy, a mixture of pines, maples and oaks filtered the light down through the pine boughs and sparkled on the water and the mica in the rock. On afternoons when he stayed later he could hear the spring peepers calling for mates.

Jonathan sat with his knees pulled to his chest and his arms wrapped around them. Watching some movement at the far side of the pond, he became aware he was not alone. He was not alarmed, just mindful. He turned to his right as Tog stepped from the trees into the small gravel clearing where years of winter had scarped loose parts of the rock.

"Just passing through or are you lost?" Jonathan was neither surprised nor startled. Something told him it would be Tog. Who else could move up so quietly?

"Nope, not lost, Lara told me you'd be out here. Finding the cabin presented a little more of a challenge, had to ask Chief Vaillancourt. That road coming in isn't anything you're gonna find by accident."

"They tell me that's what drew me to this place. Pretty much a run down, abandoned hunting camp. Get this; I actually bought it from the Wilson estate. It was Derek Wilson who nailed me–the grandson!"

"Mind if I sit," Tog stepped up onto the rock and around behind Jonathan. Jonathan moved slightly and Tog sat down pulling one knee up and draping the other leg over the front of the rock.

"Looks like the ankle is doing well."

"Hardly know it ever happened. Once in a while if I turn too fast, but hell, I don't have to do anything too fast." Tog reached down and rubbed his ankle and adjusted the pant leg down over his boot. "So fill me in. Greta said you called, but that you didn't say much else. Sorry about the phone."

"It's going well, I guess. I think Lara and Lucy; maybe even Anne Vaillancourt expected more. Too many unknowns, so they are whittling away a little bit at a time." Jonathan draped his legs over the rock and then stretched his arms behind him. It's funny, some days I'll go to look for something and I know right where it is, or do something and I know how, but then Lara will say something or ask me something and I haven't a clue."

"What's the doctor say?" Tog turned and sat on the edge of the rock.

'Not much really. Writes it all down and then adjusts something and we move on. Usually he seems positive albeit uncertain. He has said, repeatedly, that the effect of that drug is generally short term, but never really defines short term." Jonathan turned toward Tog.

"It's awkward at times, I mean the first time I walked in on Lara undressing it embarrassed me and I backed out. Lara understands most of the time, but then she'll forget and ask me something and is reminded by the blank look on my face. I know who they say I am, who I was and I know who I am, but I can't get all the wires connected in between."

"How are the girls?"

"Lucy's fine. She gets it that it's a work in progress. Lynn wants someone to wave a magic wand and make everything better–I'm told she always did. The whole thing is disturbing, actually scary at times, but like you said: slow and easy wins the race."

"It takes more strength to admit you're weak than to admit most anything else," Tog adjusted his position on the rock. "Being strong doesn't mean you don't fear things it just means you fear them in a different way. I don't want to beat this to death, but let me tell you two short stories about being strong enough to recognize your vulnerability."

"When my brother and I were in high school we were the two biggest guys. I was even a little bigger than Wynona. When he died it crushed me, I crumbled, shattered, and broken. I asked myself over and over why him and not me. But I had to stay big and stay strong for my Mom and only at night alone would I let myself cry. But Brad reeled me in and provided a safe place for me to crash and crumble. He put me back together and I moved on. Mom remained remarkably strong and she moved on, but never really recovered." Tog paused and looked out across the pond. "When Brad's wife died, not unlike me, he was shattered and broken. He too had to stay strong and bigger than life to help Kitty through her pain and loss. Bigcat and I tried to do for him what he did for me. I think we did. Sometimes the hardest thing to do is let someone care, let them in and amidst our strength allow ourselves to be weak, to lean, to be vulnerable, and to trust. It takes tremendous strength to admit a weakness–even for a moment. Enough sermon for now, but know this my friend, you are not alone."

"Maybe I knew those things before, maybe not. If I didn't I learned them well over the past couple of weeks and I thank you and Brad and others for it," Jonathan looked into Tog's eyes and then out across the pond. For a several minutes the two men sat quiet and gradually they became one with the sounds of the forest.

"We better get back to the cabin; Lara's going down to Lucy's after lunch. That's partly why I called, was wondering if you wanted some help for a few days. I apparently make one helluva Haddock chowder, you up for some?"

"Chowder, absolutely. Help sure. Company, hell yes!" Tog stepped around the rock and he and Jonathan headed down the trail to the cabin.

At the cabin, Lara was setting her bag in the back seat of the Explorer.

"Not expecting a lot of traffic, but I'm gonna try to get ahead of it."

Jonathan walked toward Lara and leaned forward and kissed her on the cheek. "I'm going up to Tog's for the weekend, you don't mind do you?"

"I think that's a good idea. Take your phone and keep it on," Lara looked at Tog with raised eyebrows. "I'll call as soon as know my plan." Lara got into the Explorer and put the window down. "Thanks again, Tog. I love you Patrick." Lara pulled her seat belt across her chest and started to back out.

"I love you too, Lara. Drive safe." Tog and Jonathan watched as Lara backed up and pulled down the drive disappearing into overhanging tree branches and green shadows.

Jonathan and Tog stepped across the small porch one step up from the moss and lichen covered ledge that made up the front portion of the foundation, past where a long woodpile was covered top only with a brown tarp. Green shutters were held back against the cabin walls and at one side of the door a wood box sat backed under an open window and at the other side two rocking chairs sat in waiting, though securely attached to the cabin with a chain and hook on each.

◊

*So, there it is, the middle, but there is no end just a new beginning. I'll gather in all the parts and wait for the whole. In the meantime I'll go as far forward as the headlights shine, by myself sometimes, but never alone.*

*Thanks for listening.*
*Jonathan*

www.ingramcontent.com/pod-product-compliance
Lightning Source LLC
Chambersburg PA
CBHW020444270626
47155CB00022B/1465